BULLET

LORDS OF CARNAGE MC

DAPHNE LOVELING

Copyright 2019 Daphne Loveling
All rights reserved.

No part of this publication may be reproduced, stored in a retrieval system, or transmitted in any form or by any means, without the prior permission in writing of the publisher, nor to be otherwise circulated in any form of binding or cover other than that in which it is published without a similar condition, including this condition, being imposed on the subsequent purchaser. This book is a work of fiction. Any similarity to persons living or dead is purely coincidental.

A previous, novella-length version of this novel appeared in *Wanted: An Outlaw Anthology* under the title *Rebel Ink*.

Cover design by Coverlüv

ISBN: 9781702525183

To Nigel and Petunia.
You're judgy, but you're furry. Thanks for being my office mates.

1
SIX

"Is it the number of times you've broken a man's heart?" he teases me. "Because if so, you're about to make it number seven."

I laugh in spite of myself. "No, that's not it either. Face it, you're never going to get it."

"Would you tell me if I did?" Bullet challenges. He gives me a sexy wink. "Come on, now. I bet I already guessed weeks ago."

"No, you honestly haven't," I tell him, flushing slightly.

Although he is right.

I wouldn't tell him, even if he guessed.

The name I go by — Six — is a frequent source of interest

and amusement here at Rebel Ink. Though, if you wanted to find a place where a weird first name would blend in, a tattoo parlor is probably one of your best bets. I work here as a receptionist and aspiring tattoo artist. I fit right in among Chance, Sumner, Hannah and Dez. Most of my customers hardly even blink when I tell them my name. Hell, a lot of them go by handles even stranger than mine.

Like Bullet, for example.

But so far, Bullet is the only one of our customers who's been this insistent on trying to find out what my name means. The first time he came into the shop — all leather-clad, tattooed, and gorgeous — and introduced himself, I tried to deflect his question by pointing out that his name was just as weird as mine.

But then he immediately told me his real first name is Wyatt, and that Bullet is the road name given to him by the Lords of Carnage MC. Apparently, 'road name' is what motorcycle clubs call the nicknames their members go by. If he can be believed, Bullet has an actual bullet lodged in his body. Hence the choice of monikers.

And hence why he keeps insisting I need to reciprocate, and reveal to him why I go by Six.

Bullet leans forward now, one elbow propped up on the counter of the reception desk that separates us. He's close enough to me that I can't help but notice the flecks in his golden-brown eyes. Beneath his short, dark beard, one corner of his full mouth twitches with mischief.

"I think I know what Six stands for," he murmurs in a low voice. There's an intimacy to his tone that sends heat straight to my core. Dammit, this man has no business being this hot. I swallow audibly and try to look unaffected by his words.

"Oh yeah?" I retort, but my voice comes out a little less steady than I want it to.

"Yeah," he breathes. "It's the number of times I'm gonna make you come."

Jesus. His words are so unexpected that I pull back in surprise, knocking a cup of pens and pencils off the counter and onto the floor. The clatter is loud, and I jump, pulse rate spiking as my heart starts to hammer in my chest.

"Sorry to startle you, darlin'." Bullet gives me a wicked, satisfied smirk. He glances down at the mess I've created. "You need some help with that?" he asks, lifting an amused brow.

"No, no," I mumble hastily as I bend down behind the counter to gather up the pens. I feel my cheeks flush even redder than before. Bullet loves to flirt with me when he comes into the shop, but *my God.* He's never said anything remotely that direct before.

If it was any other guy, I'd give him a piece of my mind. I might even go as far as to tell the owner, Chance, that one of his customers was sexually harassing me.

But as I pick up the cup and pens with shaking hands, I realize there's a reason I won't say anything to Chance. And it isn't because Bullet is a member of the Lords of Carnage MC — the local motorcycle club that gives our shop all of their tattoo business. It's not even because I'm afraid of getting on the wrong side of a man who's probably not used to being refused anything, by anyone.

The real reason I won't say anything?

It's because I've fantasized about exactly what Bullet just said.

Way more than six times.

While I'm still down on the ground, I take advantage of the two or three seconds where I'm hidden from view to take some deep breaths and try to come up with a smart-alecky response — one that won't reveal to Bullet how rattled I am. But thankfully, just as I'm picking up the last pen, my boss, Chance Armstrong, comes striding down the hall.

"Bullet. My man," his booming voice calls out in greeting. "Shit, you've been in here a lot lately. You here for some more ink?"

I stand up awkwardly just in time to see Bullet turn and lift his chin at Chance. "Hey, man. Yeah." He grins easily, spreading his hands. "What can I say? I got some time, and some space to fill."

"This is the third tattoo in two weeks," I point out, breathing a little sigh of relief that the subject has been changed. "I don't know how you have any more space on your body left."

For some reason, even saying the word *body* in reference to Bullet makes me shiver a little, but I try hard to ignore it.

Bullet glances at me, looking slightly feral. "Don't worry, I still got some room." He winks at me again, and my mind can't help but slide into dangerous territory, wondering exactly where he is and isn't tattooed.

A low thrum starts up on my skin, which feels almost electric. I try to ignore it, but it does no good.

"Shit, Bullet, I don't have any open appointments until later this afternoon," Chance frowns, glancing at the clock on the far wall. "I guess I can fit you in though, if you want to come on back."

"Actually," Bullet replies easily, "I was thinking Six could do the tat."

What the *what?*

"Me?" I ask in surprise. I glance uncertainly from Bullet to Chance. "But... I mean... I'm still in training."

"I trust you," Bullet murmurs. "You've been training with Chance for a while now, right? He wouldn't have taken you on if he didn't have confidence in you."

Actually, Chance took me on as a favor to Hannah. She started out here as a receptionist, too. Chance didn't know me from Adam (or Eve) when I first walked in the door to Rebel Ink. I've worked my ass off to pay him back for taking a chance on me, learning everything I could and taking all the grunt jobs just to show him how thankful I am. So far, he's never had any cause to complain about me. He's even said once or twice that I'm a quick learner, and that I have a good eye.

Still, it's one thing to do a simple flower on some twenty-year-old girl's ankle. It's entirely another to ink a member of an outlaw motorcycle club. I could completely ruin Rebel Ink's reputation with the MC if I fuck it up. If Bullet's tattoo turns out bad, and one of the other Lords asks about it, that would be enough to harm the shop. Which is why I look again at Chance, hoping like hell he'll refuse.

But instead, he just gives us a brief nod and shrugs.

"Sure. I'll have Dez come out and man the phones," he says swiveling on his booted heel. "Come on back, Bullet. I can come in and supervise Six while she works."

Desperately, I cast around in my head for some excuse to say no. But before I know it, Chance and Bullet are already walking down the hall toward one of the free rooms.

With a helpless sigh, I stand up and follow them, stomach already churning. On the way down the hall, Chance stops by Dez's room and tells him to go out front and man the desk for me.

Then, almost before I know it, I'm sitting on a stool, with Bullet in front of me.

Looks like this is happening.

Well, shit. Here goes nothing, right?

2

SIX

Bullet shrugs off the patched leather cut he's always wearing and tosses it on a counter.

Then, without any ceremony, he reaches up over his head with one arm and pulls his black T-shirt off over his head in one fluid motion.

"Chance knows the tat I want," he says casually, and points to a spot low and to one side of his ripped abs. "We talked about it before. It's gonna go right here."

Holy hell...

Everything has happened so quickly. I'm totally unprepared for the sight of Bullet's naked chest and torso right in front of me. I've been apprenticing with Chance for months, and I'm no stranger to seeing people unclothed. Tattoo artists see a pretty wide variety of naked body parts — for better or for worse. Old, young, fat, skinny — I thought I'd seen it all by this point. I've observed and even worked on plenty of chest and back tattoos for guys and women alike. Part of the job involves keeping a professional distance from sights like this.

For the most part, that's been pretty easy. Like how gynecologists get to the point where they probably don't see the hoo-has they examine as anything other than just part of the whole reproductive system. I mean, staring at vajayjays all day has to make them seem pretty uninteresting after a while, right? Just a biological reality, nothing more.

But *this*...

Well, let's just say my body's reaction to seeing Bullet shirtless is a little more intense than I expected. Since I'm already recovering from our earlier flirting session, my skin is still sort of tingling from his *how many times he's going to make me come* remark. Now, faced with the reality of his ripped, half-naked body right in front of me, so close I can touch it — and the fact that I *am* about to actually touch it — I'm feeling all sorts of hot and bothered.

I can barely hear anything through the roar of blood in my ears. The thudding of my heart is so loud I swear it's audible to everyone in the room. I swallow with difficulty, then try to arrange my facial features into an expression of professional indifference. As I try to get my racing pulse under control, I take a few seconds to examine Bullet's tattoos. Maybe if I just concentrate on the artwork itself, I can distance myself from how fucking hot the canvas is.

Like Chance said earlier, Bullet is already covered in quite a bit of ink. Most of it is absolutely beautiful work. Tons of people come into the shop with all sorts of poor quality tattoos, but that's definitely not the case here. I can instantly tell that

Chance has done a lot of these designs, just by the style and the degree of skill and precision. Both of Bullet's arms are covered to the wrists in intricate sleeves. Across his torso is a repeating pattern of skulls and razor wire. Lower down, on his *incredibly muscular and delicious* stomach (*okay, calm down, Six, and concentrate, for God's sake*), the razor wire snarls together to form another, larger and more intricate skull.

It's incredible stuff. So beautiful I could happily let my eyes play over the artwork for hours — regardless of the taut, muscled body underneath it.

But *good lord*. The way his ink accentuates the carved sculptural perfection of Bullet's body is a thing to behold in itself. And unfortunately for me, his tattoos only emphasize how perfectly tempting it would be to reach out and trace the outline of his tapered abs and hard, muscular chest. An almost irresistible desire to let my hands roam over him wells up inside me. I'd do almost anything to find out for myself whether this man feels as good as he looks.

My breathing grows shallow as I fight against the thoughts that threaten to overpower me. Being so close to Bullet for the next hour or so is going to be pure fucking torture. I open my mouth, in a last-ditch attempt to get out of this, but then snap it shut again like a fish. There's nothing I can do or say that won't make me seem like a weirdo, and make Chance pissed at me. There's no way to talk Bullet out of this without compromising my job. I just need to suck it up and do the tat. That's all there is to it. It's a professional challenge, nothing else. I'll have more of them in the future.

Though it's hard to imagine another tattoo in my whole career will ever be *quite* as challenging as this one's going to be.

"Okay, then!" I squeak, hating how I sound. I clap my hands on my thighs. "What's the design we're doing?"

Chance turns to Bullet. "We still doin' what you talked about last time?"

He nods. "Yeah. The bullet."

"I'll go grab the stencil."

"A bullet, eh?" I manage to smirk. "Appropriate."

"Yeah," he replies, a little gruff. "Been meaning to get this one for a while. It's gonna go right there."

Forcing myself to act cool and unaffected, I lean in to take a better look at the spot he's indicating. He shifts in his seat to give me better access. The tattoo is meant to go on his right abdomen, over the external oblique muscle. Moving closer, I see he has two long scars across his skin at the site, which are not yet covered by any ink. They look like they maybe could be from a knife. There's also a long, strangely-shaped furrow along his back and around to his side.

"It's still in there," he tells me, "since it was too close to some organ or other to take it out."

I swallow nervously. I guess he wasn't kidding about having a bullet in him. "You want me to tattoo scar tissue?" I croak.

"Just at the edge, here." He runs a thumb along the end of the scar. "At the entry point."

"You're pretty nonchalant about having a bullet in you," I remark, trying for humor. "Is that something that happens to you often?"

Bullet has always been so easy-going and charming around me that I'm expecting his usual flippant reply. But what comes back at me instead lowers the temperature in the room by five degrees.

"Only once."

His voice drops to a dark, menacing register. All semblance of flirtation between us instantly evaporates into thin air. "The man who gave it to me is dead now."

Instantly, I freeze, shocked by the abrupt change in his demeanor.

"Wow," I manage. "That's... unlucky for him."

"No," Bullet bites out, his jaw turning to stone. "He's the lucky one."

I have no idea what that means. But I don't dare ask more. I doubt he'd tell me — and even more than that, I'm almost certain I don't want to know. For the first time, I get a glimpse of the dangerous man beneath the joking, laid-back exterior. I've mostly ignored the leather biker cut that Bullet always wears into the shop, except to briefly wonder what it means to be a member of the Lords of Carnage MC. I mean, sure, I know there's probably stuff they get up to that's not exactly legal. Given my own past, I can't really judge anyone for that. But this is the first time I've come close up to the grim reality of what club life might be like. What Bullet's life is like.

I'm not sure how to feel about the fact that the evidence of that violence is right here. Under my touch. And that I'm about to tattoo a visual representation of that violence indelibly onto his skin.

Taking a deep, calming breath, I shut my mouth and try to pretend the last thirty seconds didn't just happen. Instead, I get to work prepping. I set out the paper towels I'll need to wipe his skin. Ink cups. Ointment. Rinse cup. Sterilized tubes. Needles. Razor. When my table is prepped and I'm sure I have everything I need, I grab the alcohol from the counter beside me and set to swabbing the skin where Bullet's ink will go.

Under my touch, the rigidity of his muscles slowly begins to ease. I work in silence, feeling the moment of tension between us begin to slip away as well. The tightness between my shoulder blades eases up a bit, and I allow myself a small sigh. I'm still hardly *comfortable* being this close to him, but I'm thankful to have something to keep me busy and my mind occupied. It's still a struggle to ignore the raw sexiness of Bullet's naked torso, though. Why couldn't he have wanted a bicep tattoo? Or maybe his calf? Something that wouldn't have required him being shirtless? Something a little less... *lickable.*

Above me, Bullet chuckles low in his throat as I swab up toward his ribcage. "Tickles," he rumbles.

In spite of myself, I can't help but snort. "Really?" I glance up. "You don't exactly strike me as the ticklish type."

"I'm not, normally." One corner of his mouth lifts. "How about you? I bet you're one of those chicks who's ticklish all over."

Back to the flirting, I see. I finish up and reach for the disposable razor to shave the area. "That's privileged information," I deflect.

"Yeah? You gonna make me find out for myself?" He leans forward, until his warm breath is tickling my ear. "I can do that."

Without warning, my throat lets out this weird, rabbit-like *yelp* as I pull away.

"Uh, okay, we're all prepped!" I say in a strangled, giggly voice. "I'm gonna go get that stencil now. Just sit tight!"

Standing up so quickly the stool scrapes noisily against the floor, I scurry out of the room and down the hall. Chance is just coming out of the room where we keep the thermal-fax.

"Here's what he wants," he says, showing me. "It's not that complicated, except for the shadowing."

I take a look. Even though I'm still a jangle of nerves, the tattoo itself makes me breathe a little sigh of relief. The bullet is a little larger than life-size, and rendered very realistically. The only tricky part is that it's designed to look as though it's hovering about an inch away from the surface. If I do it right, the shadowing will make it look as though it's just about to pierce the skin.

I can do this, though. I'm good at shadowing. It's one of the things I've worked hardest on.

"Okay," I breathe. "This looks easy enough."

"Don't be nervous," Chance tells me, reading my mind. "You got this, Six."

We go back to into the room, where Bullet is sitting patiently. I suck in some air and force myself to pretend he's an old, ugly, gross guy.

Then, for the next forty-five minutes or so, I focus on doing the best damn version of this tattoo possible.

As I settle in, the familiar vibration of the tattoo gun starts to soothe me, and everything else begins to fall away. There's nothing like the experience of creating a piece of art that's designed to be forever etched into someone's skin. Even the simplest tattoos, if they're done well, have their own sense of movement. The way the patterns and shapes and colors dance is unique, as is the way they accentuate the body and tell a story. The person's body becomes a canvas, their skin a work of art in and of itself. The ink on my own body has become a part of me, as much as my hair or my nose or my smile. It's as much a window to my soul as my eyes. If you know how to read it, that is.

Creating such an indelible marker of a client's identity is something I take more seriously than almost anything else. I know that's part of why Chance has kept me on and agreed to teach me. He feels the same way about tattoo artistry. And I know he wouldn't have anyone on staff at Rebel Ink who didn't.

When I've finally finished Bullet's tattoo, I'm sweaty and trembling. But in spite of myself, I have to say that I totally rocked the result. The bullet looks almost like a photograph. The shadow is so accurate that you'd swear it was right above his skin, suspended in a crucial, inevitable moment in time. I hand the mirror to Bullet so he can take a look. He stares at it for a couple of seconds, then lets out a low whistle.

"Damn, girl," he grins, giving me a nod. "I should have had you doing my work all along. Chance, you've got competition."

Chance shrugs. "She's got talent, for sure. Sometimes it's the stuff that looks the simplest that's the hardest to do." He looks at me. "You should take a picture of that for your portfolio."

Feeling almost dizzy with triumph now that it's over, I take out my phone and do exactly as Chance says. Afterwards, I get Bullet's tattoo dressed and bandaged, then recite the aftercare instructions I know by heart at this point. Bullet listens patiently. I can tell he's just humoring me, but at least he doesn't interrupt.

"Okay, dude," Chance says to him when I'm finished. He raises his hand and gives Bullet a fist bump. "You're good to go."

"Thanks, man. See you soon."

I walk with Bullet up to the front. Dez, sitting at the reception desk, looks up from his sketch notebook when he sees us. He shakes his hair back from his eyes. Then, with his typical non-verbal communication style, he stands, gives us both a nod, and disappears into the back.

I settle into the chair behind the front desk and tell Bullet the price for the tattoo. He pulls out a few bills and sets them on the counter in front of me.

At first, I think he didn't hear me right. There's at least twice as much here as he owes. I open my mouth to tell him so when he cuts me off.

"That's a tip, babe," he says. "And if you're thinking of turnin' it down, I got a way you can pay me back."

I frown at him quizzically. "I can pay you back by just giving you your money," I point out.

"Nah. Your money's no good with me," he grins.

I can't help but laugh. "You're a confusing man, Bullet."

"I'm a simple man, Six. With simple wants." He leans forward. "And right now, I want you to agree to have a drink with me."

"You ask me to go out with you every time you're here," I retort, brushing him off.

"Yeah, I do," he agrees. "And I'm gonna keep doin' it until you say yes." Bullet cocks his head and gives me that golden stare of his. "So let's just cut to the chase, huh? Come on, Six. One drink. Live a little."

Live a little.

The words resonate in my head. He doesn't know the half of it.

I live like a hermit here in Tanner Springs. It's true. And that's by design. The whole point of coming to such a sleepy town was precisely so I *could* live. Under the radar, and avoiding detection. This place has been really good for that.

But his words hit home a little harder than he can know.

Because the truth is, I *want* to go out with him. And because somewhere along the line, my life has been reduced to not much more than just existing. Other than coming to work, and a very rare girls' outing with Hannah, I have no social life at all.

That's the way I wanted it. It's perfect for me. It's how I survive.

But I am lonely. And I'm tired of spending every evening staring at the TV. Alone, and trying not to think about a future filled with nothing more than an endless stream of nights just like that one.

And here, right in front of me, is a man who just won't take no for an answer. That should piss me off. I should tell him in no uncertain terms to back the hell off. But it doesn't. Not at all. It makes me nervous, yes. But not angry.

Because if I'm honest with myself, Bullet makes me feel things I haven't felt in a very long time. Every time he has asked me out — even though I always refuse — a flutter starts deep in the pit of my stomach. A flutter of excitement. Of possibility. Of things that could be possible, if my life were a different one.

That alone should tell me he's someone I should be running far away from.

But for some reason I don't refuse him automatically, like I have every other time. This time, instead of telling him no like I should, my stupid pie hole opens, and what comes out of it seals my fate.

"Okay," I half-whisper. "One drink. And then you let it drop. Deal?"

"One drink, Six. And then," he winks, "we'll see what happens next."

3

BULLET

Damn, that girl is wound tighter than a two-dollar watch.

Even though she puts on a big show like she's untouchable, I can tell there's something else going on with her. Six has got a wall around her so thick I can almost see it. She doesn't let people get close. Why, I have no idea.

But if I only get one shot with her, I'm gonna make it count.

Having Six do my new ink turns out to be a genius fuckin' decision. And not just because she ended up doing a hell of a job. It finally kicked this flirtation we have going into overdrive and got her to let down her defenses, just a little. She was so flustered by the end of it, I saw my opening, and went for it. And damned it if didn't pay off.

Not that she was the only one having trouble controlling herself back there. Hell, just having her that close to me made my blood run hot in my veins. And I knew just as soon as I yanked off my shirt that she was feeling the same way. God damn, the way her breath hitched in her throat, it sent a jolt straight to my dick. If Chance hadn't been right there, God knows what would have happened next.

The whole fuckin' thing was an exercise in torture, for both of us. The only thing that distracted me from my own discomfort was how much I enjoyed watching Six get all hot and bothered. As I drive back to the clubhouse on my bike, I replay the scene in my head. How she trembled a little bit right before she first put the needle to my skin. Under her touch, the familiar sting of the needle transformed into an erotic thrum — a pleasure/pain sensation that buzzed from the surface of my skin straight to my dick. I had to shift myself in that goddamn chair more than once to adjust the pressure on the fucking club between my legs. It wouldn't go down, no matter what I tried to think about to distract myself.

Her lips — Six's ripe, cherry-plump lips — were parted in concentration as she worked. Her mouth was close enough to my abdomen that I kept picturing her slipping down to her knees. In my perfect world, I would have unzipped my jeans and let out the beast that was fucking throbbing for her touch. Her lips would have slipped, velvety, around my shaft, her mouth hot and wet... God damn, the prick of that tattoo gun was nothing, next to the agony of my pulsing dick fucking begging me for relief.

By the time she was done with my ink, I was already tryin' to decide whether I needed to head back home to jack myself off, or go straight to the clubhouse to have one of the club girls take care of things for me. I know the sexual specialties of every single one of them, and normally I pick and choose depending on my mood. Trouble is, not one of the club girls can hold a candle to Six in the looks department. And it's her throaty laugh that's ringing in my head as I leave Rebel Ink. It's her baby blues I want to see looking up at me as her lips wrap around my dick.

I let out a low, tortured groan. Nah. The club girls aren't gonna work for me tonight. My cock wants Six. No one else. And for once, I'm gonna wait. Steak instead of hamburger, like they say.

I'm havin' trouble not grinning like an idiot when I pull into the parking lot of the Lords of Carnage clubhouse, thinking about the fact that I'm finally gonna get her alone for a while tomorrow night.

But my good mood doesn't last long.

Tweak comes striding up to me the second I walk through the clubhouse door. "I found him," he calls out. "I finally found the motherfucker for you."

He's been working on this for me for so long, it takes me a second or two to figure out what the hell he's talking about.

Then it clicks.

"Holy motherfucking shit," I breathe.

"Where?" I ask him, still trying to wrap my mind around what Tweak is telling me.

"Here." He points at a spot on a map on his computer screen. I scoot closer in the wheeled chair, peering at the place he's indicating. "Pittsburgh," he confirms. "Or just west of there, to be exact."

"That's in Death Devils territory," I remark. "Ain't it?"

Tweak bobs his head once in a brief nod. "Yeah. And coincidentally, Oz and his men are on their way here right now."

The Death Devils are an MC to the east of us. Their prez, Oz, has a daughter named Isabel, who's our brother Thorn's old lady. The relationship between the Devils and the Lords is somewhere between rivals and allies. The last few years, they've been moving further to the east into Pennsylvania, taking territory as they go. They've been helping us with moving product and defending our turf when they can, and vice versa. So these days, we're more friends than enemies.

"What are the Devils coming here for?" I frown.

"They're on their way out to Indy," Tweak says. "Their club's stoppin' in here for a night to break up the trip. Angel's opening up the clubhouse for 'em to come party and stay for the night. Gesture of good will, shit like that."

"Indianapolis?" I repeat, puzzled. "What the fuck business they got all the fuckin' way out there?"

Tweak lifts a brow. "Fuck if I know. Thorn told me Oz used to be part of a club based outta there. I guess that club's defunct now. But Thorn seems to think the visit's got something to do with that. Even Iz doesn't know much about it, I guess. So it's probably not just old home weekend."

I nod. Isabel is Oz's only child. If she doesn't know what's going on, it's definitely not anything to do with family. It's gotta be club business. Which means Oz ain't about to tell anyone outside the Death Devils what they're up to.

Frowning, I shake my head, irritated that I've let myself be distracted from the business at hand. "Okay, well anyway, fuck that. Tell me more about what you got about Ellis. How did you find the sonofabitch?"

Tweak shrugs. "Wasn't easy, I'll say that. Sorry it took me so long. The Lords have had a lot on our plate lately, and Angel's had me running a lot of intel. I could only do this when I had time, here and there." He pauses, and cuts me a look. "It is possible this ain't him," he cautions me. "But I think I got the right guy. If it is him, he goes by Edge now."

"Edge," I snort, rolling my eyes. "For fuck's sake."

"Yeah," Tweak agrees. "Don't know if he changed his name to stay out of sight. But the pictures my contact got of him look pretty close to the one you gave me."

"You got pics?" I repeat, impressed. "Let me take a look."

Tweak hits a few keys on his computer and a folder comes up. He punches another button, and a series of photos appears, in a carousel. He flips through them, just slowly enough for me to take them all in. They're grainy and rough, some black and white and others color.

But that's him, all right.

Ellis Strickland.

My piece of shit stepfather.

The sight of his all-too-familiar face — sharp, angry eyes, hooked nose, ears set too low on his head — makes my stomach roil in disgust. "That's the fucker," I growl. "You got him."

In an instant, the last memory I have of my mother while she was alive flashes in my mind. Her emaciated body, lying on the floor of the filthy hole they lived in, head propped up on a stained sofa pillow. Her skin, waxy and yellow from the drugs Ellis sold. The drugs he gave her to keep her addicted and submissive — so submissive that they were the most important thing in her life.

And in the end, the instrument of her death.

Ellis killed my mother, just as surely as if he'd held a gun to her head.

Almost unconsciously, I reach down to finger the spot under my T-shirt on my torso where the gauze protects my new ink.

What are the odds? The very fucking day I finally get around to getting this bullet tattooed on my skin — the bullet that marks the last time I tried to kill Ellis — Tweak would finally track the motherfucker down?

The tattoo is an external marker of the actual bullet inside me. That bullet will never leave my body. It's a wound that will never completely heal. A pain and anguish I will never forget.

Until I end Ellis Strickland, that is.

A dry, bitter husk of a laugh escapes my throat. I never knew before that a laugh could hold no humor in it at all. Only disgust, and loathing.

The prison sentence I got as a result of the events of that night took my freedom for two long years. It gave him another reprieve from paying for what he'd done. By the time I got out, he had disappeared without a trace.

It's taken far too long to find the bastard. To be honest, I'd almost given up hope. The trail had run too cold. I figured maybe some other person with a vendetta against Ellis Strickland had managed to get to the sonofabitch before me. It tortured me, though — the thought that someone else got the pleasure of sending him out of this world before I could do it myself.

But now I know. He's still alive.

And with that knowledge, every emotion I've ever had to swallow — every roar of fury from deep in my soul— comes racing back, like it all just happened. The thirst for vengeance, deep and familiar, parches my throat. Anger and rage that I've kept tamped down for years shoves its way to the surface, threatening to consume me.

More than anything, I want to jump on my bike right this fucking second. Drive to where my piece of shit stepfather is, and ram the barrel of my Glock right down his fucking throat.

But even as I fight to cut through the rage-filled haze fogging my brain, I know in my black soul that the revenge will be sweeter if I bide my time. Shooting is too good for that motherfucker. I spent two years locked up behind bars, with nothing to do but dream of what I would do to him once I got out and found him. Now the moment is here. And nothing will take away the pleasure of making my face the last thing he sees as he leaves this world.

"I'll be right back," I growl at Tweak. "I'm thirsty as fuck."

I head over to the bar and bark at the prospect to set me up with a bottle and a couple of shot glasses. A couple minutes later, I'm back in Tweak's command center. Straddling my chair again, I set the glasses down next to one of the monitors and pour us both shots of whiskey. I shoot one down my throat. Then another. I'm gonna need to take the edge off before I hear this. No pun intended.

"Okay." I finally slam my glass down on his desk. Turning toward Tweak, I lean back and set my jaw. "Tell me. Start from the beginning. And don't leave out a single fucking detail."

4

BULLET

T weak accepts his shot and tosses it back easily. Grunting in satisfaction as the liquor burns down his throat, he gives me a single nod. "Okay. So you want the long story. Here it is. But it's gonna take a bit."

True to his word, he launches into an accounting of where he's been looking, what he's been looking for, and how he finally hit pay dirt. Tweak's a Lord of Carnage, but he also lives part of his life in a virtual world of dark web shit — a world the rest of us don't know a hell of a lot about. He's a fucking genius getting information from various people he knows, anonymously or not, throughout the world.

Even so, he says it's been tougher than he thought to turn up anything on the man who used to be my stepfather.

"I figured from everything you told me about him that he's the kind of guy who wouldn't venture that far outta the region, even if he was tryin' to stay hid," Tweak explains. He stretches back in his chair, cracking his neck. "So I've been lookin' around Ohio for the most part, and into neighboring states. I've been pulling in some favors here and there, so I've had guys sniffing around, seeing what they could find. I figured based on what you told me about this asshole, once a meth head, always a meth head. So I had my guys looking for him in those circles." Tweak curls his lip in disgust. "Eden had some suggestions for me, too. People she remembered from back in the day — people she figured were still around and doin' the same fucked-up shit they were when she was using."

Eden is Lug Nut's old lady. Lug Nut and I were patched into the Lords of Carnage at the same time, so we're pretty tight. Eden's also the sister of Gunner's old lady, Alix. The two sisters are originally from Virginia. Eden and Alix ended up here in Tanner Springs after Eden was kidnapped by a dirtbag who pretended to be her boyfriend. He got her hooked on drugs with the plan of pimping her out to his other shitbag friends. Alix followed her out here to look for her, and she ended up meeting Gunner by chance at the Smiling Skull when she was there searching for Eden. The Lords ended up getting involved (long-ass story), and rescued Eden from the pieces of shit who were holding her. We brought her back here, and Gunner's ma Lucy helped Eden detox. By the time it was all over, Gunner and Alix were together — and so were Eden and Lug Nut.

"Eden end up giving you anything useful?" I ask.

"Yeah. Turned out she did. She pointed me toward a guy who used to run with her ex. One of my guys went to see him, and he ended up giving us some actionable intel. He recognized Ellis from the photos. He was the one who told us the fucker goes by Edge now. Said he'd fucked off to Pittsburgh after one of the bigger dealers he was trying to take business away from ran him outta town." Tweak grins. "That was the missing link we needed to locate him."

"So, you got an address for him?"

Tweak's grin fades. "Nah. That's where we're still falling flat. Those pics on my computer are from a security cam at a roadhouse outside of Pittsburgh. Taken a couple weeks ago. My contact gave the manager a hundred bucks for the footage. But the manager says Ellis, or Edge, ain't been in there since that night. No one else he talked to at the place had seen him or knew where he was, either. Seems like he just faded into the background. But my contact says from what he's heard, he doesn't think the fucker could've gone far."

"Someone tipped the bastard off that people were looking for him," I guess.

Tweak grunts in approval. "That's what I'm thinking, too."

"In which case, we bide our time. Wait for the snake to come out of his hole. Or figure out a way to get him to let his guard down. Lure him out in the open."

I chew over this thought.

A rising commotion and unfamiliar voices outside in the main room tells me the Death Devils have arrived. Raucous laughter reaches my ears, and a couple seconds later, the music on the sound system gets a fuck of a lot louder.

"We may have caught a lucky break. If Edge" — I snort at the name — "really is where we think he is, he'd be in Death Devils territory, or just outside it. Which means Oz might know more about him. Or be willing to help us find out."

Tweak taps his forehead. "Great minds think alike."

"Speaking of which," I say, rolling my shoulders, "let's get out there, before Oz and his men drink up all our booze."

Tweak stays behind for a bit, to shut down his computer and secure everything. Not that the Death Devils ain't trustworthy, but they ain't Lords. I saunter down the hallway toward the noise, and run into Angel, our club president, just as he's coming out of his own office.

Angel lifts his chin at me. "Tweak talk to you already?"

"Yeah. Just talked to him. He told me he located my stepfather."

Angel nods. He knows the story. At least enough of it for him to be okay with me putting Tweak on it in his spare time. "You know the club's got your back on this, brother."

"Yeah. I know." I pause. "Turns out he's in Oz's territory, Tweak says. How's that for a fuckin' coincidence?"

"Could work out good for us. You talk to Oz about it?"

"Not yet." I smirk as we enter the main room of the clubhouse and I spy the Death Devils prez over by the bar. "He looks a little busy."

The club girls are all here, no doubt called on by Angel to provide a warm welcome to our guests. Three of them, Melanie, Bree, and Tammy, are hanging on Oz like he's the second coming. Melanie, with her white-blond hair, Bree's darker look, and redhead Tammy are like a fuckin' sex catalog for him to pick from. But it doesn't look like he's planning on choosing just one.

Angel barks out a laugh. "Let the fucker get his stress release. I ain't ever seen him unclench like this before."

"Right?" I chuckle. I glance over to a table a few feet away from Oz, where Thorn and Isabel are talking to a couple of the other Death Devils. "You think Iz is enjoying her dad playing harem?"

Angel snorts. "My guess is she's used to it."

We wander over to the crowd and greet the Devils one by one. Angel steps aside to say a few words to Oz, and I wait for him to finish. Meantime, I say hello to Isabel, who's wearing nurse's scrubs and looks like she just came from work.

"Hey, darlin', you're a sight for sore eyes," I greet her. "Haven't seen you around in a while."

"I've been taking on a few extra shifts at the hospital to help out one of the other nurses," she smiles. She reaches up and pulls an elastic band from her hair, which falls around her face in a dark mane. "I figured I'd come say hi to Dad while he's in town." She scrunches her brow in an irritated look. "Do you know, Thorn had to tell me he was coming? He couldn't even call his own daughter to let me know he'd be in Tanner Springs."

"Ah, he just knew I'd let ya know," Thorn tells her in a soothing tone, catching her around the waist. "No harm done."

"He sure seems to be enjoying the local entertainment," Isabel shoots back, rolling her eyes.

"Well, now, not every man is lucky enough to have a good woman by his side," Thorn teases her. "Those of us who do are blind to such lesser pleasures."

Isabel laughs, but gazes up adoringly at Thorn. "You flatterer."

"No flattery if it's true, *Sibéal*," he murmurs, kissing the top of her head.

"Okay, that's enough," I bark in disgust. "Jesus, you two are even more of a spectacle than Oz with those club girls."

"We're only getting started, brother," Thorn tosses back, grabbing a high-top stool and pulling Isabel onto his lap.

"That's my cue," I mutter, and address the two Death Devils next to them. "Save yourselves, while there's still time."

I turn away from the table, Isabel's laughter following me as I make my way over to Oz. Angel is just leaving, and I take advantage of the moment to get the Death Devils president's attention.

"Oz," I nod to him as I stride up.

Through his dark, salt and pepper beard, he actually gives me something in the neighborhood of a smile. I'm so surprised my jaw almost drops. I ain't ever seen Oz smile before, for any reason. Guess our club girls are doing their job.

"Bullet," he greets me, as Bree glides a red-nailed hand over his chest and giggles. "I almost didn't recognize you without the cue ball look," he observes.

I run a hand over my head. "Bald was cold, man. Especially in winter. Decided to grow it back out." I nod toward the women surrounding him. "Looks like you got your hands full," I remark.

"Not yet," he deadpans. "But soon."

That gets a chuckle out of me. "You got a couple minutes to talk?"

For a second, Oz is silent. Then he cuts his eyes at Bree. "Leave," he says to her and the others. "But keep your engines running."

Melanie and Tammy give him a little scowl of discontent, but slide away without a word and go over to the low couches in the corner. Bree leans over and whispers something in Oz's ear, then does the same, sashaying away for maximum effect.

"Well?" Oz asks mildly, signaling to the prospect behind the bar for another drink. Always a man of few words, is Oz.

"I don't know if Angel talked to you about this, but I could use your help on something. I'm looking for a man named Ellis Strickland. Apparently, he goes by Edge now. Tweak's been doing some sniffing around for me, and sources are saying he's been sighted around Pittsburgh recently."

One of Oz's brow raises just a millimeter. "I don't know the name. What's he doing in Pittsburgh?"

"Not sure. I'm guessing drug dealing. Last time I saw him, he was cooking meth. If so, he's probably dealing it in your territory." My stomach sours at the memory. I pull out my phone and show Oz the one photo I have of Ellis. It's a snapshot that was taken with my mom about a year before she died. "He's about forty-five, forty-six. This picture of him is old, but he looks about the same now, just grayer hair. Tweak can give you something more recent — security cam footage from a roadhouse outside the 'Burgh."

"Why are you searching for this man?" Oz's brow creases.

It's on the tip of my tongue to say, *none of your business*. But this is the president of the Death Devils. Our allies. He doesn't command the immediate respect from me that my own club's president does, but he isn't someone I want to piss off. And I'm asking him for a favor, to boot.

"He used to be married to my mother. He got her hooked on junk. She died of an overdose, because of him."

I don't tell him the details, and skirt over the actual reason she died. I leave out the meth fire. How she had to be identified by dental records. My chest squeezes, and I fight back the familiar rage that wells in my veins every time I think about the hell my mother's last few minutes of life must have been. Nausea mixes with rage deep in my gut as I fight to keep my emotions off my face.

Oz's eyes are locked on mine, inscrutable. "Is your mother the woman in the picture?" he asks, nodding toward the phone.

"Yes."

He blinks. Then, with a slight frown, he mutters, "Have Tweak send me photos, and everything he knows."

"Thank you," I say. Then I pause.

"I want my face to be the last one he sees," I tell Oz. I assume my meaning is clear.

He nods. "Understood."

Turning, I nod toward the club girls, who immediately jump up and swarm back toward Oz. I make my way to the other end of the bar, and bark at the prospect to bring me a beer and a shot. I should be feeling good — after all, I'm finally close to knowing where my mother's murderer is, after all these years. But instead, all the hatred I've been stuffing deep inside me has come boiling back to the surface. All the anger and darkness I've pushed down. All the dreams of hearing Ellis Strickland scream for mercy at my hands. All the times I've lusted to be the one to see the final light of life drain from his eyes.

I toss back the shot that appears in front of me. And then, suddenly, through the haze of blood lust that threatens to consume me, a face appears.

Not my mother's face. But Six's.

The guarded look in her dark, kohl-rimmed eyes. The mass of sexy blond hair that frames her face. The twine of tattoos around her lithe, feminine arms. She seems as though she comes from another world. One that still holds some beauty. And a shred of innocence.

Six is the only thing that keeps my mind from losing itself completely in thoughts of blood and pain as I pile on one shot after another throughout the evening. Seeing her tomorrow is the sole event on my horizon that anchors me to a world that promises more sunlight than darkness.

5

BULLET

The next night, I pick Six up from Rebel Ink on my bike at the end of her shift. She's wearing a hot little skirt with black boots, and a plain white T-shirt, under a leather jacket that's two sizes too big. The look says innocent girl and hot, sassy woman all in one. Her blond hair flows wild and loose around her shoulders. Jesus Christ, Six always looks good. But tonight she looks literally good enough to eat.

And I'm hopin' that by the time the night is over, that's just what I'm gonna do.

"You gonna be okay riding a bike in that skirt?" I ask,

noticing my voice sounds a little hoarse. She just smiles and lifts a shy shoulder.

"I'll be fine," she tells me, one corner of her mouth lifting, too. "If I can ride a bicycle in a skirt and tights, I'm pretty sure I can manage to sit on a Harley."

I'm not sure how comfortable she is with motorcycles, but when I hand her the helmet I brought for her, she takes it from me and straps it on wordlessly. I note with satisfaction she's not one of those chicks who fights wearing it because she's worried about her hair or some bullshit like that.

Six asks me where we're going as I fire up the bike, but I tell her it's a surprise. The Smiling Skull is a little ways away, a couple towns over, and I don't want her to balk and ask me to take her somewhere closer. It's a nice fuckin' evening out, and I'm in the mood for the open road.

I'm also in the mood to feel her tits snuggled up against my back for a while.

Ever since the first time I met Six, I've known she had a thing for me. God knows she's hot as fuck, and I'd hit that in a heartbeat. But like I said, she puts out this closed-off vibe — a guardedness that comes off her almost like a force field. I could tell coming at her straight-on would never get me where I wanted to go. So at first, whenever I went into the tattoo parlor, I'd just play it cool. To get the lay of the land, so to speak.

Little by little, she started letting her guard down with me — just a moment at a time, here and there. I started to flirt with her a little, to try to loosen her up. A couple times, I pushed a touch too hard, and she'd close up again like a flower at night. So, I'd back off and try again later. Eventually, I got her to the point that she'd even start to banter with me a little.

Sometimes I'd even manage to make her laugh. The first time I heard it, the low, sexy rasp in her throat went straight the fuck to my dick. Her honey-blond hair would fall back away from her face as she threw back her head, and I'd get a full-on view of how goddamn gorgeous she was.

And somewhere along the line, I made it my personal mission to get this girl into my bed.

Six never mentioned a boyfriend — or a girlfriend — and once or twice she said something about living alone. So I figured I had a good shot, with the right mixture of persistence and knowing when to give her some space to breathe.

I gotta be honest, though. Even though I've asked her to come out with me each of the last three times I've been in the shop, it took me by surprise when she finally did say yes. I figured I had at least a month or so to go before she let down her defenses and gave in. But yesterday when she was doing my new tattoo, something must've shifted inside that head of hers. 'Cause after she was done, she got all quiet and pensive and shit. And then when I asked her out — more out of habit than anything — she finally said yes.

And I am not the kind of man to waste a golden fuckin' opportunity when it presents itself.

Six gets on the bike behind me and puts her feet on the pegs without being told. When she wraps her arms around me, though, she does it with hesitation — like maybe she hadn't thought this part through all the way. But in the end, she settles in. I goose the engine just a little bit, so she'll have to cling onto me a little tighter for balance. My cock stirs as I feel her breasts press against my back.

I can't stop the chuckle that escapes my throat as she does. *Fuck yeah.*

As we ride out of town, I can feel how tense her body is behind me, and how hard she's trying not to get any closer than she has to. But after about five minutes, she starts to relax. I can tell by the way her body moves that she's starting to look around at the scenery as we fly down the highway.

Experiencing the road on a motorcycle gives you a feeling

of freedom like nothing else. I can feel Six's breathing deepen as we ride along — like she's trying to pull all the sights, sounds, and scents into her and hold onto them.

I get it, little girl.

After about half an hour, I pull off the road into the parking lot of the Skull. I cut the engine and wait for her to get off. She takes off her helmet and hands it to me. Her hair is disheveled from the ride, giving her a just-fucked look that makes me want to bend her over the seat and do what comes naturally. My cock jumps to attention at the thought.

Down, boy. Wait for it.

"Smiling Skull," she reads, looking up at the sign above the door.

"You ever been here before?"

Six shakes her head. "I don't get out of town much."

"I got that impression."

"Is this a biker bar?" she asks, glancing toward a row of bikes at the far end of the lot.

"Something like that." I raise my chin toward the entrance. Actually, the Skull is owned by the Lords of Carnage. As we go inside, I lift my chin and wave at Jewel, the manager and head bartender, who's standing behind the bar. Jewel is my prez Angel's old lady. She used to bartend at our clubhouse, back in the days before they got together. The two of them just had a kid, a little boy named Timothy.

"Hey, there, heartbreaker," Jewel calls to me easily. I notice her eyes slip to take in Six with curiosity. I don't blame her. I've never come in here with a woman before.

Left with one, yes...

"Hey, Jewel," I lift a finger at her, then point toward the back of the bar. "We're takin' a table toward the back. Send a couple of beers our way, would ya?"

"Will do."

"You a regular here?" Six asks me, eyeing Jewel with something that might be jealousy.

"You could say that," I chuckle. "Come on. Let's grab a seat. Beers should be over in a second."

Service is good for us Lords at the Skull, of course, since we own the place. It is primarily a biker bar, and we do what's necessary to keep it neutral territory, like the old owner Rosie did. We get all kinds in here, but the staff who stayed on after Rosie sold us the place keeps the rowdiest customers in line. And we have some of the Lords come in from time to time, to serve as unofficial bouncers. Tank and Striker, standing over by the dart boards right now nursing their beers, are two of them. Tank catches my eye, and I lift my chin at him in silent acknowledgment.

Six and I slide onto our chairs at a high-top table near a bay of windows. A minute or so later, one of the waitresses, Kylie, comes over with our drinks. She's Hale's old lady. She and Hale have been together for less than a year, but I guess they've known each other since high school. They reconnected down in Ironwood, where the other chapter of our MC is. Hale went down there on a job for a couple weeks, and somehow he ran into Kylie there. I'm not clear on all the details, but when he came back up to Tanner Springs, Kylie was with him, and they've been together ever since.

"Thanks, darlin'," I nod at her as she sets our bottles on the table.

"No problem," she smiles. Her eyes go to Six with barely concealed curiosity, just like Jewel's did. "Hi, there," she says, sticking out a hand. "I haven't seen you at the Skull before. I'm Kylie."

"Six," Six murmurs, smiling shyly and shaking with Kylie.

"You from around here?"

"No." Six's eyes dart away for a second as she shifts in her seat. "I mean, not originally. I work at Rebel Ink, over in Tanner Springs."

"Oh, sure. I know the place well. Is that how you two met?" Kylie asks.

Six's eyes flicker again. Kylie doesn't seem to notice it, but I definitely do. Probably because I already have some idea how skittish she can be about some subjects. I know Kylie's just being friendly, but I don't want this girl to start closing up again. After all, the main reason I brought her here in the first place was so I could finally get her to let down her guard with me.

"Thanks, Kylie," I grunt. "We're good here for now."

Kylie flashes me a look, one brow raising, but she doesn't push it. Instead, she gives us a final smile. "Just holler if you need anything," she tells us, and moves away to help other customers.

"Cheers," I say, lifting up my beer.

Six raises hers, too, and clinks it against mine. "Cheers."

I take a long drink, watching her out of the corner of my eye. It's a little quieter in here than usual, which is good. Sometimes this place gets a little out of hand for a first-timer. "So. Tell me about yourself, darlin'," I say when she puts her beer back on the table. "You ever gonna tell me why they call you Six?"

"*They* don't call me Six," she half-smirks, tilting her head at me. "*I* call me Six."

"Okay. *You* call you Six," I correct myself. Interesting turn of phrase, though. I file it away for later. "I guess I never actually asked what your *real* name is, Mystery Girl. You gonna tell me that, at least?"

She waits a beat. For a second, I think she's gonna do it. But nope.

"If I wanted people to know that, I wouldn't call myself Six," she finally says.

"Noted," I murmur.

Shit. This girl isn't gonna make anything easy, is she?

"So, where you from?" I try instead. Boring, but safe.

"Um..." Six glances down at her beer. "Nowhere, really. I was born in Western Pennsylvania." She gives me a slight shrug. "But I don't have any connections there anymore, so... It's not really home."

I frown. Seems like that was the wrong question, too. All of a sudden, Six's whole demeanor has slammed shut tighter than a safe.

Well, damn. Here I thought her agreeing to go on a date with me meant maybe she was finally gonna start loosening up. I start to get kind of pissed, but when she looks back up at me, there's something in her eyes that tells me she's not just doing this to fuck with me. She's being vague for a reason, not to be a tease.

I get the feeling that wherever she came from, she wanted to cut all ties when she left.

Hell, that's something I can understand.

But damn if that ain't gonna make this little getting-to-know-you date a fair amount more challenging.

Shit, I've never had to make this much of an effort to get into a girl's pants before. If anything, the game has gotten boring as hell. Most chicks take one look at my ink and my cut, and that's all she wrote. There's a hell of a lot of women out there who are dying to take a walk on the wild side. And my reputation does a lot of the work for me, too.

The devil that sits on my left shoulder whispers in my ear, *What's with you, Bull? Why are you trying to pry open this oyster, when there's so many goddamn other fish in the sea?*

And I guess that's true.

But even though I can't put my finger on it, I feel like finessing this little oyster might just be worth the trouble.

Something tells me that if I work on it long enough, there just might be a fuckin' pearl inside.

Taking a swig of my beer, I glance around the room. My eyes drift over toward the pool tables, and I notice there's a free one. It gives me the beginnings of an idea. A way to get Six's overly vigilant mind occupied with something else.

"You play pool?" I ask, taking a stab in the dark.

"M-hmm," Six says noncommittally, taking a sip from her glass. "A little."

"Come on, then," I say, standing up. "Let's go see what you got."

"What?" She looks up at me with a quizzical expression.

"There's a table open over there," I reply, waving my beer in that direction. "We may as well jump on it before someone else takes it."

I wait for her to stand, and let her take the lead as we walk over to the tables, trying to suppress the grin on my face. At least this way, we'll have something to focus on while we talk. Maybe I can get her to open up a little more.

And in the meantime, I can stare at her ass.

6

BULLET

Ten minutes later, we're in the middle of a round of Eight Ball. I suggested a game with easy rules, since I don't want Six to spend the whole time worrying about whether she's going to screw up and hit the wrong ball in the wrong order.

My idea seems to work. With the distraction of the game in front of us, Six eventually starts to get a little more chatty. As we play, I get her to tell me how much she likes working at Rebel Ink, and that Hannah, her first friend in Tanner Springs, was the one who got Chance to give her the job. Six does respectably well at the game. She doesn't sink the eight ball by mistake, and ends up losing to me with just two more of her stripes on the table. She has a pretty good eye for where to put the shot, and I do my best to just let her play and not give her advice. I know from experience that chicks don't always like that shit.

When the game is over, I notice she's done with her beer. I go to the bar and signal to Jewel I need two more. When I come back, Tank and Striker have wandered over to the pool table and are chatting her up.

"You trying to horn in on my date, you motherfuckers?" I growl.

Tank snickers. "Just trying to figure out what you had to do to convince a hot chick like this to give you the time of day."

Six accepts the beer I hand her, tossing her mass of blond hair over one shoulder. "Persistence, mostly. He's been asking me out for weeks. Finally wore me down, I guess." She gives me a coy look.

Striker whistles. "That's probably the only way this ugly mug manages to get any action. It sure as hell ain't his sparkling personality."

Six giggles. "He's not so bad, when you get used to him."

"That's what you think," Striker retorts. "He farts like a motherfucker when he's drunk, fair warning."

"Not helping, Strike." I shoot him an irritated glance.

But Six actually looks amused. "Is that true?" she asks, eyes flashing with merriment.

"Nah, he's fucking with you."

"The hell he is," Tank butts in. "Those farts could smoke a skunk out of its hole, I swear to God."

"Shut it, brother," I warn, as Six erupts in peals of helpless laughter.

I'm about to tell them to fuck off and leave us alone when shouts ring out at the other end of the bar, over by the door. The four of us turn toward the sound. A rough-looking dude who looks like he's had a few too many throws a punch at another guy, who ducks it and rushes him, plowing into his torso and ramming him against the wall. The first guy yells out again and pushes off the wall, bringing them both to the floor. A small crowd starts to form around them, yelling and hooting.

Tank groans. "Fuckin' idiots. Looks like we got a fight to break up."

Striker lifts his chin at me and gives Six a wink. "You watch this one," he says to her. "And remember about the farts."

"Saved by the bar fight," I groan as they walk away. "Jesus Christ, those two are annoying as fuck."

"They're funny," she protests, giving me a little eye roll. "I liked them. I think I've seen the one with the long hair at the shop before."

Then, just like that, Six flashes me an easy, carefree grin that about melts my cold, black fuckin' heart.

Well, I wanted to get her to loosen up. Looks like those two motherfuckers helped me out, after all. Better not look a gift horse in the mouth.

Though Striker is gonna pay for that fart remark.

"Yeah," I sneer, but more for form's sake. "They're funny like a sexually-transmitted disease." I motion toward the pool table with my bottle. "So, you wanna play another round?"

Six pauses a second, then crosses her arms and gazes up at me speculatively.

"What?" I ask, frowning.

"Wanna play One Pocket?" she asks with a saucy little tilt of her head. The tiniest hint of a smile twitches on her lips. It's cute as hell.

And something inside me just about comes undone.

Because I know a come-on when I hear it. Even from this little girl, who tries to play it so cool, like she's not fazed by anything or anyone. Even if she doesn't quite know it herself. Or hell, maybe she *does* know it, but she's tryin' to pretend otherwise. Either way, I'm not gonna question it. I know when to roll with an opportunity when I see one.

"One Pocket, eh?" I ask, trying to ignore the fact that my cock just got as hard as my pool cue. "You sure are full of surprises, Mystery Girl."

She cocks her head at me. "Are you really gonna keep calling me that?"

"What, you don't like the nickname?"

Six snorts. "Aren't nicknames supposed to be shorter than a person's actual name?"

"Well, I don't actually know your name," I reason. "Maybe it is."

Six purses her lips. "Point taken," she concedes.

"So, One Pocket. You certain you're up for that?"

"Sure," she shrugs. She lifts the beer to her lips and takes a drink. "I'm feeling pretty warmed up. Feeling good about my chances."

"That right? So, you want to make a wager out of this, then?" I raise an eyebrow. "Make it a little more interesting?"

"Okay," she smirks. "How about…" She pauses for a few seconds, tapping a finger on her chin. "How about, the winner gets to make one request of the loser? No questions asked."

"One *request*?" The chuckle that comes from my throat sounds wolf-like, even to me.

"One demand."

"Anything?"

"Well…" she hesitates, then gives a little shrug. "I mean, anything *legal*. But yeah, anything."

What in the hell? She's pretty much done a complete one-eighty in the span of a couple minutes. Is it the beer talking? But Six doesn't seem like she's tipsy. Far from it. Her eyes look clear and totally sober — and a little saucy. Like she's teasing me. Challenging me to take the bait.

This girl has a reckless streak I didn't see coming.

If she thinks I'm gonna waste this win on asking her what her real name is, she's nuts.

"You sure you don't want to wager something else?" I ask her, giving her one final chance to back out in spite of myself. "'Cause you're playin' with fire, little girl."

"You haven't beat me yet," she points out, reaching up to flip her blond locks behind her back.

"Okay, then," I nod with an incredulous laugh. "You got yourself a bet. Game on."

WELL, shit.

I should have known this chick wasn't gonna bet something so risky unless she was sure she had the upper hand. Turns out, Six is some kind of goddamn aspiring pool shark, and she was fucking with me the first game. I'm usually good at sussing out that shit, but damned if she didn't just play me.

We each take one of the corner pockets on the table, hers diagonally opposite from mine. I let her break, thinking I'll give her a head start. She then proceeds to run the first four of her balls, and just barely misses the fifth, turning the table over to me.

In the process, she's done a reasonably good job of positioning two of her other four balls near her pocket. That keeps me from taking any low percentage shots. I'm no fuckin' slouch at pool either, though, so I sink the first of my balls easily. The second one is a little trickier, since I have to do a bank shot that might backfire on me. As I lean down and eyeball it, Six wanders into my field of vision and makes a show of chalking her cue, wiggling her ass right behind the ball and causing my cock to jump to attention.

"You're doin' that on purpose," I growl, noticing that my voice has turned hoarse.

Six glances over her shoulder and flashes me a knowing look. "Is it working?"

"Goddamn, girl," I mutter under my breath. "You better hope like hell I don't win."

I had been planning to only ask for a kiss as my prize, to let her off the hook. But her sass is starting to give me ideas for revenge.

In the end, though, she edges past me and sinks her last ball while I still have two on the table. It's only when the ball plunks into the pocket that she drops the mask of cool detachment she's been wearing since the first shot. She does a little hop into the air and pumps her fist, with a dance that ends in another shake of her ass. It's ridiculous, and cute as hell, and sexy to boot. I'm tempted to burst out laughing, but also to bend her over the pool table right here and now, other people be damned. My cock needs relief after watching her sexy little body parade in front of me this whole game.

I don't do any of those things, though, because I'm also pissed that I just lost. It's been a long damn time since anyone's beat me at pool. I sure as hell have never been smoked by a woman before. I'm doing my best to take it in stride, but I'm failing. Especially because I also just lost a bet I was fucking sure I'd win not even fifteen minutes ago.

"Two outta three?" I growl.

Six laughs and shakes her head. "Nope. That wasn't the deal."

"Okay, then," I shrug. "Fuck it, I ain't gonna argue. You won fair and square. Even though you took me for a ride, you faker. I should have guessed you were better than you let on."

"Damn straight I was," she says smugly.

"All right, all right," I mutter. "No need to rub it in. Come on, I'll buy you a shot and you can tell me what your demand is. You did say anything *legal*, right?"

I'm disappointed as hell but trying hard not to show it as we belly up to the bar. Jewel pours us each a shot — Jack Daniels Tennessee Rye for me, tequila for her. "On the house," Jewel says with a smile. She nods at me and gives Six a wink before moving away.

"Thanks, darlin'," I call after her, then turn to Six. "Okay, so. You won fair and square." I raise my glass in a toast and salute. "Congrats. Why don't you tell me what you won?"

Six picks up the glass and tosses back that shot of tequila like a pro. I watch her long neck as she swallows, my cock aching at the thought of what she could do to me with that mouth.

And then, to my utter amazement, she leans in to whisper in my ear.

"I'm gonna let you take me back to my place, cowboy," she murmurs, the faint aroma of agave tickling my nostrils. "That's what I win. As long as you agree to stop asking me what my name means once and for all."

"That's two requests." I manage to choke the words out while my dick is yellin', *Hells, yeah!*

"Don't get smart," she says breathily. "Now, let's get out of here, before I change my mind."

SIX

I hear myself laughing as I climb onto the back of Bullet's bike and put my feet on the pegs. I listen to my voice as I tell him my address, and hope that I'm the only one who hears the slight tremble in it.

I want this. There's no question about that. Being around this man — staring at his damn sexy, teasing eyes as they look me up and down, watching his muscles flex under his shirt as he aimed for a shot across the table — I should have known I wouldn't have a chance in hell of resisting him if I allowed him to take me out. It's been even harder to keep my cool tonight than it was when I was leaning over the taut muscles of his abdomen giving him his tattoo.

There's no way around it: this man oozes sex. And without the protection of the front counter at Rebel Ink, or the supervision of my boss Chance's watchful eye, I'm a goner before I even realize it. All it took was a little alcohol to break down the last of my reserves. That, and the tantalizing sense of power I had from knowing that I was in control of that pool game just now. I could feel his eyes on me, watching my body as I moved around the table. I knew Bullet liked what he saw. The flood of pleasure overwhelmed my senses, knowing he was seeing me in control. Sure of myself. Sexy.

It was intoxicating. It made me want to be what he saw in me: Free. Happy. The kind of girl who isn't always looking over her shoulder.

All of the things I used to feel about myself.

At the same time, I'd be lying to myself if I pretended I'm not afraid of what's about to happen between us. As much as I want it — and oh, God, do I want it — the reality is that it's been an eternity since I've been with a man. It's been so long, I can hardly stand to let myself think about it. No matter how I try to give Bullet the impression that I'm cool, calm, and in control of myself, I'm nervous as hell right now. Nervous in a way I haven't been since my very first time having sex. My brain is crying out that this whole thing is a huge mistake, even as my body is telling it to shut the hell up and let it have a little fun for once.

But I'll be damned if I'll let Bullet see this war that's raging inside of me.

As we fly down the highway back toward Tanner Springs, I can't help but admire once again the sure, deft way he handles the powerful motorcycle under us. It doesn't seem possible, but the way he maneuvers the bike, so strong and capable, turns me on even more than I already am. Between my legs, I can tell my panties are already soaked through. I push down my embarrassment and try to hold on to my *cool, collected* persona, even as I can feel I'm starting to come a bit unraveled.

By the time we get to Tanner Springs, I'm a mess of hormones and barely-suppressed desire. Not a moment too soon, Bullet turns onto my street. I point past him to the nondescript apartment building I call home. He pulls up in front of it and backs the bike up against the curb. I hop off a little awkwardly, holding onto his hard, muscled shoulder for support. A second later, the bike's engine dies and he's standing in front of me.

Once I've pulled my helmet off, Bullet's eyes land on mine. "You ain't changed your mind, have you, Six?" he rumbles.

The smoldering look he gives me makes it clear he knows damn well I haven't, but I give him credit for making sure all the same. I don't even respond. I just look up at him through lowered lashes, then turn and on my heel and head up the front walk. I know he's watching as he follows behind me, so I put a little extra swivel in my hips, enjoying the dance of seduction that I haven't done with anyone in so long. Somehow, the dance calms me a little — makes me feel more like I'm the one in the driver's seat. For now, anyway. Because I can tell just by looking at Bullet that once we're in bed, he'll be the one in charge.

If he fucks the way he handles a motorcycle, I'm in for the ride of my life.

"You just move here?" Bullet frowns as he looks around my barely lived-in living room.

I sweep it with my gaze, trying to see it as he would. There aren't any pictures on the wall. Objects on any surfaces are strictly utilitarian. The flowered sofa and mismatched chair are Dumpster-diving treasures. The soft, plush area rug in the center of the room is the only touch of luxury in my otherwise spartan decor.

"No," I admit, self-conscious. "I've been here a while. I just... don't care a lot about knick-knacks and artwork and stuff, I guess."

The more stuff I have to pack, the harder it is to leave quickly if I have to.

I shrug off the oversized leather jacket I'm wearing. It was a parting "gift" from my ex-boyfriend that I shamelessly stole from him when I skipped town in the dead of winter a couple of years ago. I should really get rid of this thing, given all the bad memories it carries with it. I almost have, a couple of times. But something has always ended up stopping me. In a way, I wear it almost like a shield. I feel like it reminds me to always stay alert and on my toes. Another layer of secrecy between me and the world.

Bullet takes a step toward me. "You're a woman after my own heart," he jokes, seemingly satisfied with my response. In spite of myself, I tense up. Bullet doesn't seem to notice, though, as he pulls up on the hem of my shirt and slides it up my stomach and over my head. Tossing it on a chair, he takes a step back to look at me.

"Nice ink," he murmurs appreciatively. His rough, callused fingers start to trace the serpentine lines of the artwork that covers most of my right shoulder and arm. They're patterns I designed — mostly abstract, but still full of meaning for me. He reaches around and undoes my bra, and I let him, shivering slightly as the cool air hits my breasts.

"You're fuckin' gorgeous, you know that, Mystery Girl?" he rasps. Bullet's right hand comes up to cup one breast, to tease the already hardening nipple with his thumb. When I suck in a shuddering breath, his eyes slide up to meet mine.

"Good?" he asks.

I nod, swallowing around the nervous lump in my throat. "Very."

He leans down to graze my lips with his. "Shame we waited so long to do this," he says, taking me into his arms. "We've got some lost time to make up for."

My skin is alive, clamoring for more of his touch, but a far-off alarm bell is sounding in my head. "Wait!" I let out a little yelp, putting a hand on his rock-hard chest to hold him off. "You, um, know this is just a one-time thing, right?"

"Yeah." He chuckles. "Don't worry, Six. I ain't gonna cry into my beer if you don't call me afterwards." His laughter reassures me, and I feel myself relax as he backs me up against the wall. "But remember what I said about your name."

Bullet's hands slide around my ass as he pulls me to him. He's already hard as steel, and I stifle a moan, my eyes fluttering half-closed. "What's that?" I gasp, even though I know what he's going to say. I just want to hear him say it again.

His lips brush against my neck before moving to my mouth. "It's the number of times I'm gonna make you come. So buckle up, Mystery Girl."

THE FIRST TIME I come is right up against that wall. His hand slips under my skirt, between my legs, and finds my soaking core. The low growl of his voice resonates through my entire body as his lips continue to tease and devour mine. "Fuck, Six," he groans. "Jesus, that's sexy. You're wet as hell, you know that?"

I start to stiffen up at his words, but then dimly through the haze of my own desire I remember he said the word *sexy* and make myself relax again. "I... It's been awhile," I admit in a strangled half-whisper.

"Then let's make it count." His finger moves aside the fabric of my panties, expertly locating my clit. As his tongue finds mine, he begins to stroke, in slow lazy circles that make me dizzy. The rhythm of our tongues follows suit, establishing a connection that starts my whole body vibrating. Something about the way he's touching me paralyzes me, and all I can do is clutch onto his shoulders as he holds me against the wall and continues his assault. I'm helpless to do anything, my entire body a prisoner of the pleasure he's giving me. I hear myself whimper softly, my hips rising and straining toward his hand on their own. Before I realize how close I am, I'm already coming, shuddering against his chest as I ride the waves.

Then I'm in his arms, and he's carrying me through the hall. I fight through the haze of my orgasm and try to find the words to direct him to my bedroom, but by the time I do he's already there, shoving aside the tangle of sheets and bedcovers to set me down on the mattress. Then my panties are off and the skirt is at my waist, and he's lying down on the bed below me, his head between my legs.

His tongue finds my sensitive nub, already swollen from coming, and swipes gently at it. I cry out, the sensation riding the edge between pleasure and pain. Bullet backs off a bit, but grabs my hips, pulling me to him. He starts to lap at me again, softer this time, careful to build the pleasure again by teasing just enough to make me want more, then more still. Somehow, he seems to know my body already — just how much to push me before backing off, just how to help me climb the mountain of my need — until I'm whimpering and straining toward him, desperate to fly over the edge once again.

This time the orgasm is deep, earth-shattering. It feels like my whole body is exploding, the pleasure radiating outward to every nerve ending, engulfing me in its power.

My head is still thrown back against the mattress as I feel it move underneath me. Bullet's eyes are dark and hooded as he kneels between my legs. He's naked now, his cock full and hard and pulsing. He reaches down and strokes the head against my throbbing pussy. I gasp at the heat of it, the slickness against me. Instinctively, I start to angle my hips up to him, then I freeze.

"Do you have protection?" I whisper. I pray the answer is yes, because at this point I'm not sure I can stop myself either way. I *need* to feel him inside me.

His only response is to hold up two fingers. A shiny square foil package is between them.

I watch in fascination as he opens the wrapper and slides the condom down his large, thick shaft. Just seeing his hand on himself like that sends a jolt of pure desire through me.

Then, he grabs my hips again and pulls me toward him. The thick head of his cock pushes inside me and I moan as the rest follows, my walls stretching to meet him.

"Fuck," he grits hoarsely. "Jesus fuck, you feel good, Six."

Six. It's good when he calls me that. It reminds me that there's still some distance between us. That there are still things he doesn't know about me. It reminds me that this intimacy between us is just physical, nothing more.

This is just sex. Just amazing sex. It's okay.

A moment later, he starts to thrust. He begins slowly, the length of him going so deep it's almost painful. But the pain, just like before, turns more to pleasure with each pull and push. My eyes open to take him in — the full, manly beauty of his body — and our eyes lock. I start to look away, but he stops me with a sound.

"Stay with me," he orders. "Oh, fuck, baby," he rasps. "Stay with me."

I do as he says. He begins to ride me harder, pumping faster, his eyes never leaving mine. I've never felt more naked, never more exposed. Having sex with him feels like a trust fall from the top of a cliff. He doesn't know my name, knows next to nothing about me, but right now he sees so far inside me that I've never been more bare to anyone else in body or soul. It's terrifying, thrilling. And from the look of sheer lust on his face

— the instinctive, animal need in his eyes — I can tell he feels it, too.

The slickness of his cock tortures my already tender clit. I stifle the first moan, but the second one rips through me, my voice joining with his as he groans my name again. From deep inside me something starts — something unlike anything I've ever felt before. I know what it is, but it's different. Deeper. Almost scary in its power.

"Bullet," I whimper softly.

"I got you, babe." He's thrusting harder now, slamming into me with a force that's driving both of us forward. "You're close, aren't you?" I can only nod as my whole body starts to shake. "Come with me, Six. Give it to me."

It's as though his words unleash a flood. I half-scream something that's not quite a word as I tense and then let go, bucking and writhing as the impact starts deep inside me and hits me like a bomb. A second later, I feel Bullet hiss my name and erupt inside me. My walls clench around him as he lifts me in his arms, and I throw mine around him and hang on for dear life. I've never imagined anything like this — the force of it as strong as a time bomb. We're both shuddering together, the two of us coming as one, and I hold onto him like I'm in danger of being swept away forever.

The blood is rushing in my ears. I'm gasping for air, my chest rising and falling. I cling to Bullet and wait for the wave to slowly recede. Eventually, my breathing starts to slow, my heart still slamming in my chest. My arms and legs feel like rubber. My whole body feels as weak as a kitten.

"That was three," Bullet rumbles, laughter in his voice. He pulls his head back to look at me, eyes twinkling. "I know you said this was a one-time thing, babe. But I gotta tell ya — I think your body has other ideas."

8
BULLET

I knew — or at least I was pretty sure — that fucking Six would be good. I've waited long enough for it that my dick has been primed for her pussy for weeks.

But Jesus fucking Christ if what just happened hasn't thrown me for a fucking loop. The second I touched her, the second my mouth closed on hers, it was like a fucking inferno consumed us both.

Until tonight, I could never quite figure out why I was working so hard to get Six to give me a chance. I've never been one to chase pussy, since pussy tends to chase me. There was just something about her I couldn't quite put my finger on. I found myself going back to Rebel Ink just to see her — to hear her voice, to watch the little flush in her cheeks when I flirted with her. It was almost like my cock was leading me there, like a missile locked on its target.

Turns out my cock must have known something I didn't. Because even as I lie here with Six, still trying to catch my breath after an orgasm that almost blew my fucking head off, I know it's not just my dick that wants her. There was something in the way she looked at me as I moved inside her — something raw, and bare, and true — that reached deep inside me. I don't know how the hell to describe it. It's never happened to me before, and I have no fucking idea where it came from.

I want to know more about her. Not just her name. I want to know *her*. I want to get inside that pretty little head of hers. I want her to trust me with her secrets, as much as she trusted me with her body just now.

It's a thought that should scare the shit out of me.

But for some reason, it doesn't.

I'M ALMOST positive Six is gonna kick me out of her bed and her apartment after sex. But she surprises me by falling fast asleep while I'm still holding her in my arms.

And even though I've made it a rule never to stay overnight with women I fuck, I'll be damned if this one doesn't feel too good to let go.

I roll her over gently onto her pillow and reach down off the bed to grab the covers that got pushed off onto the floor while I was fucking her. She doesn't even stir as I pull them over us.

As I lift up the sheets over her shoulder, her blond hair falls to one side, revealing a small tattoo on the back of her neck. It's usually hidden because Six wears her hair down most of the time, but I noticed the outline of it earlier. I push a lock back further and lean forward to examine the ink.

It's a rose, small and delicately drawn. The petals are slightly open, but the thorns on the stem below are long and sharp. I blow out a soft breath through my nose as I stare at it. That's Six, all right: beautiful and tough, and trying her best to hide her light from the world. I wonder if there was a reason she got this tattoo — some particular event that made her want to mark the memory of it on her skin forever.

I wonder if there's a chance in hell I'll ever find out.

I lie back against the unoccupied pillow, my arm brushing against hers. Instinctively, she curls toward me, her body pulled by my warmth. I gather her into my arms again, something catching in my throat as I do. I know there's no way she would have done this if she was awake. *Her body trusts me, even if she doesn't.*

I wouldn't admit this to Six — or to anyone, for that matter — but I've been wanting to hold her like this for a while. I was lying to her when she made me promise I knew this was just a one-time thing. I've been hoping that once I got inside the fortress, I could stick around a while. Try to knock down a few more walls.

And judging from the way she's holding onto me now in her sleep, maybe I've got a prayer of doing just that.

I don't usually sleep very well, for the most part. Too many sins in my past, I guess. But that night I sleep the sleep of the dead. My body is exhausted and satisfied after fucking Six like our lives depended on it. The next morning, I wake up before she does. We've both moved around during the night, but she's still curled up in a little ball beside me like a cat.

My first instinct is to sneak out and give her her space. But something stops me.

Instead, I slide out of her bed, making sure not to wake her, and grab my jeans. Then I go into the kitchen to see if there's anything to eat.

When I open the fridge, I almost bust out laughing. This

girl's got even less food on hand than I do. There's almost nothing I can see in here that's edible and not expired, unless you think a breakfast of dill pickles with mustard on them sounds appetizing. I close the refrigerator door, shaking my head, and start rummaging around in the cupboards. It's pretty fuckin' sparse in there, too, but eventually I find a few things I can throw together and pretend it's a meal. Thank Christ she has a coffee maker and a bag of coffee. Otherwise, I might have ditched her then and there and gone out for bacon and eggs.

Ten minutes later, I'm back in Six's bedroom, a plate in one hand and a mug in the other. "Hey, Mystery Girl," I call out softly. "Breakfast."

Six stirs in the bed, then hurriedly props herself upright on one elbow. Her other hand goes self-consciously to the covers as she pulls them up over her breasts. "Wh... um... morning..." she murmurs, peering at me through the curtain of her hair. Her face registers confusion, a little shock, and more than a hint of shyness.

"Your kitchen is a fuckin' embarrassment," I say good-naturedly. "I figured you'd want coffee, since it's one of the few things you have on hand."

I hand the mug to her, which she takes, and set the plate on the bed. Six immediately draws the cup to her nose, breathing in the aroma, then looks down at the plate and does a double-take. "What the hell?" She gives me an odd look. "What is that?"

"Half of a strawberry Pop-Tart and some kippers on Saltine crackers," I tell her. "Hey, don't blame me. It's from your cupboard. You better hope the zombie apocalypse doesn't come anytime soon. You don't have enough food in this place to last you a day."

I go back out to the kitchen and get my own mug of coffee and my plate of disgusting breakfast. I come back to Six and sit down on the bed next to her, noticing she's taken a nibble of the Pop-Tart. "Who does your grocery shopping for you, anyway? I haven't seen kippers since my granddad was alive."

She takes a sip of the coffee, grimacing a little. "Damn, that's hot. My dad used to like them." She shrugs. "I guess I must have gotten a craving for them at some point and bought a couple tins. I didn't even realize I had them."

"You mean these have been in there for so long you've forgotten them?" I ask, raising one of the crackers up to look at it. "Am I gonna get food poisoning from this shit?"

She snorts. "Are you kidding? I think kippers are indestructible. *That* is quality zombie apocalypse food right there. Preppers probably stock these in their bomb shelters."

"So, your dad likes these things, huh?" I put one of the crackers in my mouth and chew. It's not that bad, if you like fish. "He live around here?"

"He doesn't live around anywhere," she replies flatly. "He's been dead since I was fourteen. Drove his car off the highway into a ditch when he was drunk out of his mind. No seatbelt."

"Oh, fuck." I chew some more and swallow. "I'm sorry."

"Yeah, me, too. But, not much I can do about it, right?"

It's clear from Six's sour expression that she doesn't really want to talk about this, but I decide to push a little more. "What about your mom?"

She rolls her eyes and takes a bite of Pop-Tart. "Who knows? She's a drunk. Rarely has a stable address." For a second, Six is silent, and then laughs wryly. "I guess maybe I'm more like her than I thought, in that way. At any rate, I don't know where she is. She surfaces every once in a while and calls me. Half the time she's calling to tell me she misses me and wants to see me, but it hardly ever actually happens. Last time I talked to her was about ten months ago."

"Shit, Six. That's fucked up."

"Well," she retorts, a new bite in her voice. "That's my life.

Such as it is." Her whole face grows dark as I can see her almost physically drawing into herself.

Shit.

I decide to give her a little of my story, hoping to make amends.

"I didn't have a dad at all, growing up," I tell her. "He's out there somewhere, I guess, but I never knew him." I eat another kipper. "You know, these aren't half bad. My mom was a drinker, too, at first. And eventually, a junkie and a thief for her lowlife boyfriend."

Six turns to look at me, her eyes wide and interested. "Really?"

"Yeah. I've been in the MC lifestyle since I was about sixteen or seventeen. Gave me someplace to be that wasn't home, since Mom and Ellis didn't want me there anyway. Christ knows I didn't wanna be there either."

"Can I ask how you got that bullet in you?" Six murmurs quietly, her eyes cutting to my torso. She's forgotten my questions about her family by now, and I think that's fine. Her guard is sliding back down, which is what I want.

"Officially?" I smirk. "Involuntary manslaughter."

I expect her to freak out, even move away from me. Instead, she swallows, her face paling a shade. "You mean, you've been in prison?"

"Two years in county." I nod toward my torso, and the tattoo that she marked into my skin. "I'm not eager to go back. But I don't regret what I did. The man I killed deserved it, and more."

Six is silent, contemplating my words. "How do you decide when someone deserves to die?"

"In this case?" I hear my voice turning hard. "When you walk in on him taking his pleasure with an underage girl who was drugged outta her mind."

"Jesus," she breathes. "Did you know her?"

"No." The girl's face is etched into my memory, though.

Especially her eyes. They were so fucking blue. A little like Six's, actually. Huge in her face. And so scared —terrified, actually — but so, so fucking far away. Like the drugs had locked her away, a prisoner in her own body. She was helpless to fight against them, and against the man using her for his own sick pleasures. She couldn't have been more than sixteen, I thought at the time, and I was right. It turned out she was barely fourteen. Not even a sophomore in high school yet.

She barely even reacted when the gun went off. Her half-vacant eyes just stared at me, as she slid her body away on the stained sheets, toward the wall. It was like she was a tortured animal, trapped in a cage.

I had come to the trap house to find Ellis. I had tracked his ass there on a tip I bribed out of a guy Ellis knew — a piece of filth just like him. I broke into the place, my Glock 27 raised and at the ready. But he wasn't there. The asshole raping that little girl was, though.

I shot the motherfucker through the back of the skull. Then I called Tank and told him to bring a cage to the address so I could get the girl out of there and transport her to the nearest hospital. I picked her up off the bed but she started to fight me, weakly, not registering I wasn't there to hurt her. While I was struggling with her, carrying her down the hall, a sudden commotion from the back of the house told me we weren't alone. I ran outside, kicking out the screen door as I went, and had just cleared the porch when a gunshot rang out and clipped me in the side. I stumbled and fell, the girl still in my arms just as three sets of red and blue rollers came screaming around the corner.

The cops hauled me in, of course. At first, they thought I was one of the guys involved with kidnapping the girl. Thank fuck when she sobered up, she remembered enough of what happened to tell them I had been the one to save her. The bullet in my side, plus the bullet in the rapist's head that matched my Glock, convinced them it was the truth.

I suspect I got charged with manslaughter instead of homicide because the parents of the girl turned out to be prominent citizens in the community. They were more than thrilled to have their little girl back — damaged, but still physically whole. I spent two years in prison. Two years waiting for another chance to find and kill my former stepfather. In the meantime, Ellis must have heard what happened, figured I was coming for him, and bugged out.

I don't tell Six any of this. It ain't the time or the place.

"Can I ask you another question?" Six murmurs, breaking into my thoughts.

"You can ask," I reply, tensing.

"What's it like being in the Lords of Carnage?"

I relax a bit, relieved. "It's a brotherhood," I say simply. "My brothers have my back, and I have theirs. We look out for each other." I pause. "The Lords are family. More of a family than I ever had growing up.

Six is silent for a moment, considering.

"It's dangerous, isn't it? Being in an MC."

I nod. "Life is dangerous, though. Question is, when you're putting your life on the line, whether the danger is worth it."

I hear her blow out a soft breath. "Good point."

Six asks me some more questions about MC life and the Lords of Carnage. I answer what I can, and tell her when I can't. I realize she's starting to warm up to me again, since she doesn't have to talk about herself.

What are you hiding, Mystery Girl?

When I've finished my food, I stand up from the bed and nod toward Six's mug. "You want a warmup on that?" I ask.

"I'm good, thanks." She hands me her empty plate and watches me in silence as I go back out to the kitchen. A few seconds later, I come back with a fresh cup for myself. "You know," she smiles shyly as I sit down on the bed again, "no one's ever made me breakfast in bed before."

"I'm not sure you can call what we're eating 'breakfast,'" I chuckle.

She laughs. "Well, anyway. Thank you."

"You're welcome. So," I smirk. "You gonna tell me anything more about you?"

She smirks back. "Nope."

"Well, then, I guess we're gonna have to think about some other way to spend the morning." I let my eyes slip down over her body. The blanket has fallen down to her waist, revealing her full, luscious tits. "Something that doesn't involve talking. You got any ideas?"

Six purses her lips. "I have kipper breath."

I take her mug and set both of them on her nightstand, then stand and undo the button and fly on my jeans. "That makes two of us," I say with a grin as I slide across the bed to her. "It's like it was meant to be."

SIX

Bullet leaves my place after telling me he still owes me one more orgasm. I laugh but don't answer him, because my mind is a freaking mess after last night and this morning.

I know it was dumb of me to agree to go out with Bullet in the first place. And I sure as hell never should have taken him home with me. I should have known my loneliness plus my dangerous attraction to him were a terrible combination. I *never* should have put myself in a position of having to try to resist him.

Because resisting Bullet is something I am apparently not very well-equipped to do.

The one thing I can be thankful for is that he doesn't take my number, or try to make plans with me as he leaves my apartment. After he closes the door behind him, I exhale, feeling empty but relieved. It's as clean a break as I could have hoped for. Except for his orgasm IOU, which I tell myself is probably just a joke.

One and done. A hot-as-hell experience. The best sex of my life. But that's it. And it's much better this way.

I turn and take a long look around my living room. Just like I've done so many times before — in other apartments, in other towns — I reflexively start a weird game I play with myself. I calculate how long it would take me to pack things up if I had to leave at a moment's notice. What I would take with me, and what I would leave behind.

Padding back into the bedroom, I grab our empty coffee mugs from my nightstand, then head into the kitchen. The coffee maker is still on, so I pour myself another half-cup and go sit down on the couch. I take a sip and grimace. It's been sitting on the burner too long by now, and tastes bitter and a little burnt. I set the cup down in disgust and scan the room again, my mind going into automatic list mode.

The couch and chair, I'd leave. Most of the furniture, in fact, since I got most of it at thrift stores or freebies people left in front of their houses. I'd hate to leave that rug, though. I love that thing. I can probably tie it to the top of my car if I have to.

Shaking my head, I heave a deep, frustrated sigh. Am I truly thinking about leaving? I know I've been in Tanner Springs too long. I can't risk getting comfortable. But the truth is, I really kind of like it here. Plus, I'm still in training to be a tattoo artist at Rebel Ink. It would be stupid to leave before that's over. I'd feel bad for Chance, who I'm sure expects me to stay on once I'm ready to do ink without supervision. And I want to. I do. I like working for Chance a lot. He's tough but cool, and he tells it like it is. I always know where I stand with him.

And the other people at the shop are great, too. Hannah counts as one of the closest friends I've ever had. She's the only person in Tanner Springs who knows my real story. One of the only people anywhere, actually. She's kept the secret that I blurted out to her one drunken night, and I've never worried she'd blab it to anyone as long as I didn't want her to. I know that if I left, Hannah would explain it all to Chance. She'd understand why I took off, without me even having to explain it to her. She'd make Chance understand, too. And hopefully in the end, he wouldn't be too mad at me for it all.

But God, I'm getting so tired of running. So tired of never putting down any roots. So sick to death of knowing that every time I set foot in a new place, it's only a matter of time before I'll be off again to somewhere else, having to start all over again.

Suck it up, Stacia. You don't have a choice. You fucked up last night with Bullet. And now you're gonna have to deal with the consequences.

A wave of sadness washes over me. Wearily, I lean back against the couch cushions, drawing up my knees and folding my arms protectively around them.

I can't help but picture Bullet's face. His dark eyes, the sexy smirk emerging through his short-cropped beard. That beard, which was softly scratching my thighs last night as he teased and tormented me to orgasm...

Shivering, I pull my knees closer. Would it be so bad if I just stayed a few more weeks? Maybe just until Chance thinks I'm finished with my apprenticeship? And while I'm here, would it be a crime if I see Bullet a few more times before I move on?

You know better, Stace. Don't go getting soft, just because of a guy. That's the kind of thinking that will get you hurt, or worse.

I know it's true. It's been a long time since I've allowed emotions to have any part in the decisions I make.

I decide to play it by ear, and stay just a little longer. Just to see what happens. I tell myself I'll be watchful, and take off at the first sign of trouble. I can do that. I'm sure of it.

I don't see or hear from Bullet that day, or the next, or the next. By the fourth day, the soreness between my legs is gone, and the memory of his touch against my skin is starting to fade. It's almost like I dreamed our encounter. I try to feel relieved that he seems to have forgotten about me. But the truth is, I'm a little sad, too.

One early afternoon, I'm sitting around binge re-watching *Black Mirror* and waiting for it to be time for me to go in for my shift at Rebel Ink. I woke up in a terrible mood, and I'm pissed at myself that I didn't go for a run or something this morning to get myself out of the house and get my mind off things. Just as I'm trying to decide whether to watch one more episode or go take a shower, my cell phone rings. I leap up from the couch and run to grab it from the kitchen table, hoping in spite of myself that it's Bullet calling me.

But it's not him.

It's a number I haven't plugged into my contacts, on purpose. But I still recognize it.

My muscles tensing, I press the button to accept the call.

"Mom," I say, my voice dull and expressionless.

There's a sort of muffled scraping sound, like the phone's being dragged across a carpet. I call her name through the phone again, louder this time. More muffled noise, then the murmur of voices far off, but I can't tell what they're saying. *Goddamnit!*

"Mom!" I yell as loud as I can, a sudden wave of rage flooding my veins. Furious, I'm about to hang up, when a breathless, barely-conscious voice replies on the other end.

"Stacia?" she slurs.

"Mom, what is it?" I bark impatiently. She's drunk. Of course she is. So drunk I'm surprised she could even figure out how to call me. There's nothing good that can come out of this conversation, I know from bitter experience. But now that I was dumb enough to answer, I just have to get through it and get it over with.

"Hi, honey," she mumbles, her voice morphing into a fake sing-song. "I haven't talked to you in so long!"

"Mom, what do you want?" I repeat, pushing down my disgust.

"Honey, I need a li'l help." *Oh, God. Of course you do. And I know exactly what kind.* "I need some money, honey. I gotta pay rent... Landlord's gonna kick me out if I can't pay 'im..."

"Mom, where are you?" I demand.

"You don't gotta come here, honey," she wheedles. "I just need you to send me some money, okay?"

"I'm not going to send you money, Mom." I brace for what I know is coming next.

"Please, honey! You have to help me! How are you not gonna help your own *mother*?" she cries out, her voice moving from coaxing to shrill.

"I'll *help* you, Mom." I suck in a deep breath and pinch the bridge of my nose, squeezing my eyes shut. "But I'm not sending you cash. If you can give me your landlord's phone number, I'll call him and figure out how to pay your rent for this month to him directly."

"You don't hafta do that! Just pay me!" she insists.

"No." My tone is clipped, final. I already know how she'll use any money I give her, no matter what she tells me. She'll sleep on the street before she goes without booze. "I will not. Give. You. Money. Period."

"Ahhh!" she half-shouts in anger. "Fuck this! You..." she starts to yell, words tumbling from her mouth incoherently. A second later, the phone goes dead.

Staring at the blank screen, I wonder for the thousandth

time how I ended up with a mother who only cares about me as someone to tap for booze money.

I haven't been in regular contact with Mom since I left the house at seventeen. Ironically, until my dad died, she was the parent who was more in control of her alcohol habit. She drank, yes. A lot, even. But she managed to keep it together and hold down a job. Maybe she was hanging on to that last bit of responsibility because she knew Dad didn't have any.

But after he was gone? It was like she started drinking in overdrive, to make up for lost time.

I have no idea where she is now. I guess I should be grateful when she calls to ask for money, so I at least know she's still alive.

Feeling suddenly cold and even more alone than I usually do, I set down the phone on the couch next to me, and hug my arms to my chest. I find my thoughts wandering again to Bullet, as they have so often the past few days. I wish he was here. I don't usually like to talk about my past, but he knows about my mom now — at least the bare bones of the story. If he was here with me now, I'd probably tell him about the phone call. And about how even though I don't want to admit it to myself, I feel guilty for telling my mom no.

Bullet told me his mom was a drinker, too. And a junkie. I realize he never said whether she's still alive. I wonder whether he has a relationship with her at all. I feel bad that I didn't even think to ask.

I stare off into space for God knows how long, lost in sad and bitter thoughts. By the time I snap out of it, it's too late for me to grab a shower before I need to leave for work. I haul myself up off the couch, feeling sluggish and depressed. For once, I'm not at all in the mood to go to Rebel Ink. Making friendly small talk with customers is pretty damn low on the list of things I want to do today. At least Hannah is on during part of my shift, which makes me feel a little better. Maybe I'll tell her about my mom's phone call, if we get a minute to chat. She's always been an amazing listener. For once, it feels like opening up to someone might do me some good.

Outside my apartment, I walk toward my car in the lot, pressing the remote unlock button on my fob as I go. Somewhere in the back of my mind, I register vaguely that I don't hear the normal click my car makes as the doors unlock. At the car, I slide into the driver's side, tossing my bag on the passenger seat beside me, and pull the door closed. I'm reaching for the ignition, key in hand, when I see something that makes me do a double-take.

The glove box. It's open.

A sensation like static rushes all over the skin on my body, as though all the little hairs are standing on end. My chest grows tight with a sudden rush of adrenaline, my breathing suddenly labored, like I can't pull in enough air.

Shit!

My eyes dart around the parking lot as I shift wildly in my seat. I slam my hand down on the door lock button, then let out a panicked squeal and swivel to look in the back seat, banging my knee against the center console in the process.

No one's there. It's okay! I'm in the car alone! Shit. Calm down, Stace! Calm! Calm! Breathe!

I can't bring myself to close my eyes, but I turn back to the front and focus on a point on the dashboard. I force myself to sit still and suck a deep, shuddering breath in. I hold it for a second, then let it out slowly. I do this a few more times, as I repeat in my head that I'm in no immediate danger.

A few more breaths, and the panic starts to subside. With a shaking hand, I reach over and rummage through the open compartment.

Insurance card, tire gauge, car cleaning wipes, a box of feminine products... It doesn't look like anything's been taken. Just rifled through.

Your insurance card has your real name on it.

Panic starts to well up in me again, but I push it back down and try to replace my terrified thoughts with more reasonable ones.

Maybe I left my car unlocked last night? I don't exactly live in the best neighborhood. It was probably just some kid wandering around, trying doors for an easy steal. A crime of opportunity, they call it. *Yeah. That's probably all it is.* I force a shaky laugh at the thought of some young delinquent boy pulling out my box of tampons.

But it might not be. It might be...

My heart starts to pound again. Even as my mind tells me I'm being ridiculous.

I've learned over time not to ignore my instincts. Usually, my gut and my head are in complete agreement on stuff like this. Whenever one says it's time to go, the other one starts making exit plans.

This glove box should be enough to convince me it's time to disappear once again. It's what I promised myself I'd do.

But this time, I feel a war starting to wage inside me.

Dammit, I've let this town get under my skin.

And if I'm honest, it's not just Tanner Springs.

It's a one-night stand with a bullet in his side, who has probably forgotten all about me by now.

BULLET

The day after I spend the night at Six's place, Angel calls to tell me Oz and his men are back from their run to Indy.

"Oz wants you to ride down to see him at the Death Devils clubhouse," he says. "ASAP."

"This about what I think it is, prez?" I ask.

"I'm sure it is. Oz said he's got intel for you. Wants to give it to you in person."

"You good with me leaving for a day or two?"

"Yeah," Angel grunts through the phone. "I think we can manage without your pretty face for a bit."

I chuckle. "All righty, then. I'll talk to ya when I get back."

The ride to the Death Devils clubhouse should take me a little more than two hours. Less if I push it. I don't bother packing much. I just throw an extra shirt in my saddlebag in case I stay overnight, and hit the road.

On my way out of Tanner Springs, a fucked-up thought hits me like a brick to the skull. My route is gonna take me past the town I grew up in. A sick ball forms in my stomach at the realization. I haven't been back to that hole since the days right after my mom died. There's no reason to go anywhere near there anymore. There's nothing there for me now. Nothing but bad memories and regrets that threaten to well up and choke me until I can no longer breathe.

I'm not sure what the fuck possesses me to do it. Maybe because of what I'm on my way to the Death Devils to find out. But whatever it is, half an hour later I find myself pulling off the main highway, to follow a familiar pitted blacktop road toward a destination I hate but can't make myself avoid.

The town I grew up in, Soldier, is a fucking shit hole. There's no nicer way to put it, and no reason to try. These days, it's got a population of probably two-hundred — if even that — down from more than three times that size at its peak. There's no reason the town should ever recover its old glory days; the auto factory that used to supply it and the neighboring towns with most of their jobs closed up shop years ago. After that, most anyone who could leave the area, did. Those who are still around live a shadow of a life, in a place that's somehow even sadder than a ghost town for the walking dead who still live there.

As I drive into Soldier, the familiar crumbling façade of the abandoned school on the edge of town greets me. It was probably a cool old building, back in the day. I'd guess it was built around the 1940s or something, but I don't know shit about architecture. The school's been closed for as long as I can remember. The few children who still live here are bused over to the consolidated K-12 school down the road. That's where I went, too. My mom moved us here when her own dad died, leaving her the house she grew up in. It was a piece of shit, like the rest of the town. But the upside was that you could live here on practically nothing — which was exactly what we had.

The main street leading into Soldier is lined with mostly shuttered businesses these days. There's still a bar, a craft shop that says it's open but never is, and a post office the size of a closet. There's not much hope here in Soldier. It's been all but forgotten by the rest of the world. The people here don't have much to live for, far as I can tell. They spend their time looking for ways to escape mentally what they haven't been able to escape physically. That's how the bar still manages to stay open, when most everything else has closed.

Soldier was the perfect place for a predator like Ellis Strickland to settle in and take advantage of the desperation.

When Ellis first moved in with my mom, he seemed like an okay guy. He worked at the auto plant, like pretty much everyone else around there. He didn't hassle me too much, and he'd give me money sometimes to go buy gas for our rusted-out Dodge so I could get out of Soldier and go raise hell in one of the neighboring towns for a few hours. Ellis was pretty good about looking the other way when a beer or two disappeared from the fridge, too, even though I was way underage.

When Ellis started bringing around some of the lowlifes he was hanging out with, my mom looked the other way. He kept the lights on, after all. And he kept her in booze, which gave her an incentive not to make too many waves. Eventually, though, Ellis started dealing drugs out of the house. It made a shit ton of sense, in a way. Soldier was so small it didn't have a local police force. And the sheriff's office didn't much bother with it, either. No better place to keep illicit activities out of sight than a town no one cared about.

Around the time I turned seventeen, shit at home had started going downhill fast. Ellis had changed from the laid-back dude he was back in the early days. Even though he was living rent-free in my mom's house, he started bitching that all she was good for was spending his money. And I was a worthless piece of shit who didn't do anything but take up space and eat up all his food.

I had started hanging around the Lords of Carnage MC by this time, with my buddy Lug Nut. I liked being away from home, and I liked the brotherhood and loyalty of the Lords. The life they chose wasn't always an easy path, but it had a code of honor that appealed to me. I tried to talk my mom into kicking Ellis out of the house, but by this time she was using as well as drinking. Her drug of choice: methamphetamine. Ellis being her supplier, she knew she wouldn't be able to get it for free anywhere else. She didn't have a job anymore, since the grain supply store where she had been working part-time had closed earlier in the year. She took Ellis's side, of course, and told me to get my nose out of her fucking business. So I did. One day, I finally had enough of trying to save her from herself, and moved out.

From just dealing, Ellis eventually turned to cooking. He set up a meth lab in the basement. My mom didn't stop him. On the contrary, he taught her how to cook, too. By that time she probably thought it was a great idea. It was a way to have her own steady supply, and not have to worry about running out. I hadn't been back to the house in over a year at that point. It had stopped being home for me a long time ago. So I didn't know about any of this shit until after it was all over.

The lab blew up one day when Mom was home alone. The initial explosion was so big it blew out all the windows on the first floor. Sparks from the fire caught the vacant house next door, as well.

There's no fire department in Soldier. By the time trucks

arrived from a neighboring town, it was way too late to do anything but just let the house burn, try to stop the blaze next door, and make sure no other houses were affected.

They found my mother's charred remains in the basement afterwards. They speculated she was down there trying to cook herself a dose when the lab blew. The cops didn't do much to try to figure out what happened. Why would they? She was just a random small-town junkie to them. They're a dime a dozen in these parts. They probably figured society was better off without her.

But I understood what had happened. And I knew who was responsible. I swore, from the moment I showed up to identify her remains, that I would make Ellis pay for her life with his own.

My mind is swirling with these bitter memories as I turn my Harley onto my old street. At the corner, an ancient-looking man I don't recognize stops to look toward the rumble of my engine, then slow-motion hurries toward his house and ducks inside. Half a block in, I roll to a stop in front of the burned-out remains of the house I grew up in. It hasn't been bulldozed. No one ever bought the land. It just sits there — a mass of decaying, rotting wood and debris. Next door to it, the partially-burnt house still stands vacant, its front door hanging wide open on its hinges.

I don't get off the bike. I don't even bother to cut the engine.

I just sit there for a moment or two. Looking. Remembering.

Bile rises to my throat as I imagine my mother, screaming for help, trapped in the flames. The pain and horror of the last moments of her life.

"I will fucking burn you," I whisper.

Then, with a squeal of my tires, I gun the throttle and leave Soldier behind, for the last time. I won't be back.

"Thank you for alerting me to your stepfather's presence in our territory," Oz intones. "Somehow he had escaped our radar until now."

Oz throws a glare at one of his crew, whose jaw tenses. I'm pretty sure the guy is the Death Devils' version of Tweak. And that Oz isn't happy with him about this lapse.

"So, what's the story?" I ask.

"It's not just drugs," Oz half-snarls. I'm surprised by the sudden sharpness in his normally emotionless voice. "Though he traffics in those as well. This Edge is involved in running a prostitution ring in the western suburbs of Pittsburgh. We understand his business model is to cater to a clientele with certain tastes that are not generally shared by the mainstream. Certain unpleasant kinks. And also a taste for youth. Girls..." He pauses, venom dripping in his tone. "And boys."

My stomach twists as I remember the bullet in my side, and the reason it's there. "I'm not surprised," I growl. "He's always been a piece of shit."

Oz lifts his chin toward the man he shot the angry look at earlier. At the signal, the man clears his throat and begins to speak.

"There is a wrinkle, though. Edge is working for the Grim Vipers."

My brow furrows. "The Philly MC?"

"Yeah. They're moving west. So far, we've avoided a turf war with them."

"Shit," I hiss. The Grim Vipers are big, and powerful as hell. Their brutality, their vengefulness and the heartlessness of their murders are the stuff of fuckin' legend. Not only that, but they've got the cops in their area on the take, too. So the Vipers pretty much do whatever the fuck they want to do, whenever they want to do it.

I know without even asking Oz that the Death Devils don't have the men or the power to go up against them. There's just no way. It would mean the end of their club if the Vipers traced any attack on them or their associates back to the Devils.

"So you need to hang back on this," I say.

Oz doesn't answer directly, but his meaning is clear. "Rodrigo will communicate with your intel man." He cuts a glance at the other guy, who bows his head in assent. "We will give you all the information we're able to find. Beyond that, I can't help you. The Death Devils can't go in with you to take Edge out. That will have to fall to the Lords. Recognize that we will help you as much as we can... from here." He pauses, his expression turning stony with anger. "But I will be happy to have this human garbage out of our territory."

"Understood."

I wonder if Oz is thinking about his daughter Isabel as he speaks. A couple of years ago, Oz hired my club brother Thorn to protect her from one of Oz's enemies — a man who had a thing for taking revenge on rivals by stealing and violating their wives and daughters. So Oz knows what it's like to have a loved one in danger, and to need help from our club to keep her safe. I figure maybe that's why he's been so willing to help me with my shit in the first place — even if he's not able to send his men into battle with me.

Sensing the meeting is over, I stand and hold out my hand to the Death Devils president. "I'll fill Angel in when I get back, and have him put Tweak in touch with Rodrigo here."

Oz invites me to stay at the clubhouse for the night and party with his men, but I'm not in the mood for that shit. I thank him again and take off for Tanner Springs, adrenaline buzzing through my veins and plans coming together in my head.

I'm close. Finally, I'm fucking close to ending Ellis Strickland.

SIX

I'm worried when I show my face at Rebel Ink after the glove box incident that Hannah will notice right away something's wrong with me.

Fortunately, I'm in luck. The shop is super busy today. When I walk in for the start of my shift, there are already three groups in the front waiting area, and two other people there by themselves. So at least for the moment, there's not going to be a lot of time for chit-chat among the employees.

"Chance just got here, so his appointments are backed up," Hannah grumbles as I hang my jacket up on the coat rack and switch off with her behind the appointment desk. "God forbid one of us should be one minute late, but I guess it's fine for Mister Boss Man."

I have to bite my lip at her snark. I know she doesn't really mean it. Hannah has adopted this attitude toward our boss mostly out of self-preservation. She has a major crush on Chance, which she finally confided to me one night after far too many margaritas and an earnest pinky swear that I would never tell a soul. Truth be told, I think Chance might feel the same about her. But he's got a strict no dating co-workers rule at the shop, and he's not the kind of boss to make an exception for himself. So instead of flirting, the two of them go back and forth with a practiced banter that seems to be their way of relieving the sexual tension between them.

"I heard that," Chance calls out, emerging from the hallway. "And for your information, I left a message on the shop's voicemail that I might be late. Delilah's mom came down with the flu, so I'm taking her this week until she's better. I had to drive her to pre-K, and the drop-off is always a freaking traffic jam."

Hannah looks chastened. "Okay, fine." She reaches up and pulls her riot of flame-red hair into a messy top knot. "But you could have texted me."

"I could have, but I assumed you'd check the damn voice mail," Chance shoots back, giving her a pointed scowl. "You know, like the receptionist who opens is supposed to do?"

"Um, receptionist? You mean, the tattoo artist who is filling in at the front desk?" she lobs at him.

"What's wrong with being a receptionist?" Chance says, cutting his eyes at me with humor. "That's kinda classist, and maybe even sexist, don'tcha think, Hannah?"

"Who says a receptionist has to be a wom-"

"Okay, kids," I say, exasperated. "Let's break this up. Y'all have customers waiting."

Chance looks like he wants to retort, but my appeal to his professionalism wins out. "Who've we got?" he asks me, tossing

Hannah one last glare before coming over to look at the computer screen.

About half of the customers waiting in the reception right now area have appointments. The rest are walk-ins. One of the appointment groups is a mother, daughter, and aunt. They're here to get matching tattoos in honor of the aunt's daughter, who died in a car crash a few months ago. They immediately gravitate toward Hannah, who takes them back into one of the larger rooms so they can all do them together and give each other moral support. Chance takes the two guys, who seem like they're here on a mutual dare. Finally, Dez comes out and greets an older man who's on his third session for a large back tattoo.

Once the three of them have taken their clients back, I set up the third group and the lone woman with albums of art to browse while they're waiting. There's a mountain of paperwork behind the desk that hasn't been gotten to yet, so I start in on that next, more than grateful for the distraction.

The time passes quickly. The woman who's here by herself eventually seems to chicken out. She stands and mumbles that she'll come back another time. I smile encouragingly at her and let her go. It's never a good idea to get a tattoo unless you're absolutely sure you want to do it, so we're not about the hard sell at Rebel Ink.

The last group, three girls in their early twenties with pouty lips and expensive blowouts, chatter at each other loudly, laughing the whole time. After a lot of consultation with one another, they each finally pick out the tattoos they want. When Sumner comes out of the back room for their appointment, they all stop and look up at him wide-eyed. Then, one by one, they each catch their breath and let out a coordinated giggle, like identical triplets.

Sumner is pretty damn good looking, to be fair.

"Okay. Which of you ladies wants to go first?" he asks in his deep baritone. All three girls' hands fly up in unison. Sumner glances over at me, one ironic eyebrow raised, and I suppress a snort. I know he'll take all three of them back at once, and flirt with them the whole time. From now on, every time one of these chicks tells the story of how they got their ink, "the hot tattoo guy" will be a major part of the story. Sumner will become the stuff of legend for this little gaggle for years to come.

A few minutes after Sumner leads his blond bevy into the hallway, Hannah emerges with the mom, daughter, and aunt. All three of them look happy, triumphant, and a little teary. I can tell right away that it was an emotional session. They thank Hannah over and over again, and tip her lavishly before they leave.

"Those poor women," Hannah shakes her head as the door closes behind them. She leans against the front counter with a sigh. One strand of her hair has escaped the messy bun on top of her head, and she distractedly hooks it behind her ear. "God. It always gets to me when someone comes in for ink to commemorate someone they've lost, you know?"

For some reason, my mind drifts to the rose tattoo on my neck. "I know what you mean," I murmur softly, reaching up to touch the spot. Hannah must catch something in the tone of my voice, because her eyes lock onto mine. "Um," I continue hurriedly, "what art did they ask you to do?"

She gives me an odd look, then continues. "A pink lily — Lily was the girl's name — with the dates of the girl's birth and death in a circle around it." Hannah flexes her shoulders and rolls her neck. "They told me all about Lily while I worked. She was getting ready to be a freshman in college this year."

"That's so sad." I shake my head in sympathy. So young, and so much to look forward to.

"Yeah." Hannah goes over to the couch in the waiting area

and flops down. "Oof. Thank God there are no other clients waiting. I need a break."

"You're not going out for a smoke?" I ask. Hannah usually spends her breaks out back.

"Nah. I quit on Saturday." She holds up an arm and pulls back the sleeve of her shirt to reveal a nicotine patch. "See?" she grins.

I congratulate Hannah and give her some quiet, turning back to the computer to finish keying in the last of the paperwork. A few minutes later, the sound of the front bell announces a new customer. Before I can raise my head to greet the person, Hannah does the job for me.

"Hey, long time no see!" she calls out. "Afraid Chance is busy right now. You got time to wait?"

"Actually, I came to see someone else," Bullet answers.

My stomach flips as I raise my eyes to meet his. Bullet comes up and leans across the counter, exactly where Hannah was a few minutes earlier. "Hey, there," he rumbles. His voice hums through me, deep and penetrating.

"Hey, yourself," I blush back. The flood of happiness that washes through me is almost overwhelming. I try and fail to keep a cool, detached demeanor. "You here for ink, or for something else?"

"Yup." He grins that gorgeous, reckless grin of his, and just like that, I'm practically a puddle on the floor.

"You know, you don't have to get a tat to see me." My words come out high and girlish. I barely suppress a giggle. *Good lord, what's wrong with me? A giggle, for Christ's sake!*

"What if I want both?" Bullet shoots back.

"Um... if you want me to do it, I think Chance is gonna be occupied for a while," I start to explain, but he stops me.

"Chance will let you do me without him watching." He lifts his chin toward the back, then gives me a wink. "Just go ask him. Tell him I'm good with it."

I toss a quick glance at Hannah, who is gaping openly at us. "I can take the desk," she stammers, giving me a look that clearly means, *You are going to tell me all about this later.*

"Uh, okay... Let's go back and ask him," I reply shakily. I lead Bullet into the back to find Chance, who just shrugs and gives his okay when Bullet tells him he wants me to do the tattoo unsupervised.

This time, the design he has in mind is a hellhound. He wants me to put it in the space just below the bullet.

As nervous as I was last time, this time it's almost worse. Because this time, the heat of his skin reminds me of what it was like to be in bed with him. I can't help but remember how I shuddered against his tongue, and then against his cock, as he made me come. How good it felt when he lost control inside me. How whole I felt. How complete.

I never told Bullet this, but I woke up once that night, and he was holding me in his arms. I wanted to pull away, but I couldn't make myself do it. I can't remember ever feeling safer than I did right then. My body still aches with the memory of how warm he was. How solid, and real. I slept better that night with him than I have in years. It was like every cell in my body knew I was protected. That nothing and no one could hurt me, as long as he was there.

It's hard to concentrate on my work, even though Bullet hardly talks the whole time. My skin feels electric, the low buzz of the ink gun almost like it's coming from inside me. In fact, I'm so nervous that I make my first mistake ever on a customer: I give one of the hellhound's eyes a heart-shaped pupil.

"Shit," I hiss. Bullet looks down and frowns.

"What's up?"

"I, uh... well, I made one of your hound's eyes heart-shaped. I can fix it," I add hastily. "It's small. I just have to..."

"Leave it," he interrupts me.

"But..." I stammer.

"I mean it." Bullet chuckles. "I can't see it. But I'll know it's there. I kind of like the idea."

"Are you sure?" I stare at him in disbelief.

"Yep." His eyes twinkle. "I won't even tell Chance you fucked up. On one condition."

"What's that?" I'm trying to sound casual, but inside my heart starts to pound.

"You let me take you out tonight."

I wish I could say I consider turning him down for even a split-second.

"Really? Bribery, Bullet?"

He shrugs. "Call it what you will."

I heave an exaggerated sigh.

"Well," I quip, keeping my voice light, "if that's the only way I can get you not to rat me out to my boss, then I suppose so."

Bullet waits patiently while I concentrate on finishing up his tattoo without screwing up again. When I'm done, I recite the spiel about aftercare that Chance makes us say to everyone, regardless of how much ink they already have or how many times they've been to our shop. When I walk back out to the front with him, Hannah is still sitting at the front desk. He pays her, and then turns and gives me a wink. "Tonight, then. What time do you get off work?"

"Seven," I murmur self-consciously, not daring to look at Hannah.

"I'll pick you up at your place at eight."

Bullet doesn't wait for an answer. He just pivots and strides out the door.

I may or may not stare at his tight ass in his jeans the whole time.

"What in the hell was *that*?" Hannah demands the second the door latches behind him. "Jumping Jesus Christ, Six! Why didn't you tell me you had a thing going on with one of the Lords?"

"I... well..." I stammer. "I don't, I mean, I didn't..." I shake my head and try again. "What I mean is, I don't exactly have a *thing* going on. It's just, he's been flirting with me for a while. And yeah, a few nights ago, I let him take me out. But I don't think it, like, *means* anything." I shrug helplessly. "Until just now, I figured he'd forgotten all about me, to be honest."

"And now?" Hannah skewers me with her eyes. "That didn't exactly look like forgetting."

"Now..." I trail off, my eyes moving to the front door. "Well, maybe we have a *little* bit of a thing going on?"

"Hot damn, girl." She lets out a low whistle. "Way to go. And here I thought you had put on your chastity belt and thrown away the key."

"So did I," I admit. "To be honest, I'm a little freaked out. I keep wondering whether I'm making a big mistake."

"Well, if you *are* making a mistake, you're sure as hell making it with the right person. Those Lords men are *hot*. Every damn one of them." Hannah sighs. "I just don't know how there can be *that* much sexy packed into one club. And Bullet's one of the hottest ones among them. Which is saying something."

Hannah seems so happy for me that it stops me from saying what's on the tip of my tongue to confide to her: that I'm starting to think I'm losing my footing a little bit where Bullet is concerned. It's like I thought I was wading safely in the shallows, and now all of a sudden the water is up over my head and can't touch bottom anymore. It's only now, when I'm so happy he's come to ask me out again I feel like I'm going to burst, that I see how much I've been trying to push down my feelings for him. This whole time I've been telling myself he's just a fun fling before I leave town. I mean, sure I've had a thing for him ever since we met, but I thought it was just because he was sex on two wheels. Now I'm starting to think it's more than that.

This *whatever it is* with Bullet is *definitely* a mistake. The more time I spend with him, the worse I feel about having to eventually leave town. He's like a magnet that's gotten too close to my compass. I feel all discombobulated around him. Like I can't figure out what direction my head is going.

I'm so lost in my own thoughts that I completely forget about my car being broken into, until I get off work and see the still-open glove box when I slide into the driver's side.

By then, it's easier to tell myself I was just overreacting earlier. Because I have more important things on my mind now.

Like what I'm going to wear for my second date with Bullet.

12

BULLET

Well, fuck. Looks like my date with Six is gonna have to wait for a bit.

I'm on my way to pick her up a little before eight p.m. when my cell phone buzzes in my pocket. I pull over to the side of the road and fish it out to see that Beast, the VP of our club, is calling me.

"Yeah," I bark into the mouthpiece. "What the fuck? This better be important."

"Hey, brother. I need you to come back to the clubhouse. We got a situation with a shipment we're driving down to Ironwood. Striker was coming with us on the run but he's stuck up north and won't be back in time. Angel needs you to fill in for him."

"What, now?" I frown. "Can't it wait until morning?"

"Nah. It's gotta be there tomorrow in the morning. They shoulda left by now, but they were waiting for Strike. They're gonna leave as soon as you show up. How quick can you be here?"

It's on the tip of my tongue to ask Beast whether someone else can do it. But that ain't the way I operate. Club business comes first. It always has. That's part of the oath I took when I patched into the Lords of Carnage. Just because it's inconvenient right now don't mean shit.

"Yeah. Tell Angel I'm on my way. Just gotta make a quick phone call. Half an hour, max."

"Sounds good, brother. Will do."

Beast hangs up. I go to the home screen and start to flip to my contacts, then spit out a curse as I realize I don't have Six's number. Well, I'm almost to her house anyway. I'll just run over and tell her in person. That way at least I get to see her for a bit.

When I roll up to Six's apartment building, she doesn't make me wait. She comes out the front door right away to meet me before I'm even off the bike. She's dressed simply, in a tight black pair of jeans that look painted on and a red tank top that matches her cherry lips. She's wearing her oversized leather jacket against the chill of the evening air. That jacket shouldn't look so sexy on her, but I dunno — somehow it works. I groan as my cock stirs in my pants. Jesus, she looks good. If I had time, I'd take her inside right now show her just *how* good.

Six sashays up to my bike, a happy, expectant look spreading across her beautiful face My chest gets tight when I see in her eyes how much she's looking forward to this date. Shit, I was, too. I hate like hell to have to leave her like this. So does my cock.

"Hey, babe," I murmur before she can say anything. I note

with satisfaction that her face flushes at the pet name. "Look, I hate to do this to ya, but something just came up. I got some club shit to attend to that can't wait."

Six's eyes grow sad, but to her credit, she doesn't pout about it or make a fuss. "Oh. That's too bad."

"Yeah. It is." I frown. "Believe me, I wish I didn't have to. But it ain't my choice. Club business."

Six pauses for a moment at my words, then nods. "Okay. Well…"

But I've grabbed her by the hand and pulled her toward the bike. Standing, I thread my fingers through her hair and tilt her head up to mine. I give her a long, deep kiss that leaves her breathless and panting. By the time I pull away, she's bright red. She gives me a dazed half-smile.

"Rain check?" I rumble hoarsely. She nods again. "Okay. Look, I need your number. I ain't gonna be back in town tonight, but I'll call you when I can and let you know what's up."

Six pulls her phone out of a small bag looped around her shoulders. We exchange numbers. When we've finished, she looks at me through dark lashes.

"I'll miss you," she murmurs. "Be careful. I do expect a rain check on this date."

"I'm always careful, babe. Don't you worry. I'll be back before you know it, and I'll make it up to you."

I fire up the engine and give her a one-finger wave, taking one last, long look at the fiery, beautiful mystery standing there. Knowing she'll be waiting for me to come back to her should feel like a burden. But instead, it feels like a goddamn present. And life is definitely not in the fuckin' habit of giving me presents. It's a new sensation, for sure.

And I'm pretty sure I like it.

I nod toward her front door and raise my eyebrows, signaling that I'm gonna wait until she goes back inside before I leave. She gives me a soft, doe-eyed smile, and turns back toward the apartment. I watch her ass until she's all the way inside.

Jesus fuck, I wish like hell I was going in there with her.

Then, cursing under my breath, I put the bike in gear and head for the clubhouse.

THE CLUB'S a little late heading out, on account of the last-minute change in plans. It's already dark by the time we get to Ironwood, the newer, southern chapter of our club. We're there to help pick up a shipment of guns from a cartel that has a base in Atlanta. The cartel runs them up to us through Nashville and Lexington. Normally, the Ironwood chapter could handle this run by themselves. But this time their prez, Axel, sent half of them on another run out to the east to deal with another problem. So Angel said we'd go down and give them a hand, since the guns are coming up to us anyway. Once they're in our possession, we'll drive them further north up into Milwaukee, to sell them to one of our contacts up there.

When we get to Ironwood, there's a party already in full swing at their clubhouse. The fact that they've got a run tomorrow doesn't seem to be slowing the party down at all. Liquor is flowing like water. Club girls run around on stiletto heels with skirts so short you can see daylight between their thighs. Axel, the Ironwood prez, emerges out of the crowd of men in leather cuts and comes out to greet us.

"Angel, brother," he yells with a wolfish grin. "What the fuck took you so long?"

"There any booze left for us?" Angel cracks back. The two presidents approach each other and clap one another on the back.

"Shit, yeah," Axel laughs, looking around at the rest of us.

"But you better get moving. My men have been goin' at it for a while. You snooze, you lose."

"Hey, stranger," coos a soft, feminine voice beside me. I turn to see one of the club girls, a hot as sin redhead I remember spending some quality time with last time I was here.

"Hey, there, darlin'," I smirk as she drapes herself across me, casting about in my head for her name.

"It's Ginger," she pouts, reading my thoughts.

"Looks like you're already jumping right in, brother," Tank grins. "I'll leave you to it." He, Striker, Hale, and the others head off to join the crowd. Angel and Beast go with Axel, no doubt to talk business before they start to party in earnest.

"It's been too long, baby," Ginger whispers breathily in my ear as she clings to me. "I missed you. Nobody fucks like you, you know that? Nobody."

In spite of myself, I'm irritated. My cock isn't in complete agreement with me on that — like I said, this chick is hot as sin — but even so. I can't pretend my cock couldn't use some servicing tonight, especially because I've been fighting blue balls ever since my date with Six got blown out of the water. But Ginger just isn't doing it for me right now. I know without even trying that if I take her down the hall into one of the guest apartments, I wouldn't be able to help comparing her to the girl I just left back in Tanner Springs. Shit, if I was there right now, I'd be getting ready to give her orgasm number six — and probably trying for seven and eight.

"Nah, not today, darlin'. There's plenty of other men who'd play, though. Go find one of them."

But Ginger ain't so easily deterred. She looks down and mistakes the swell in my jeans for enthusiasm. She licks her lips, her pout turning into a grin of triumph. "That's right, baby," she coaxes, reaching down to cup my growing erection. "See? You know you want to!"

For fuck's sake. I know from experience that she'll do whatever the fuck I want her to in bed, but I just ain't in the mood for this shit. "Goddamnit," I growl, grabbing her hand. "I ain't that hard up. Go find someone else to grope."

Her eyes flash. "You didn't think you were hard up the last time we made it!" she spits.

"Any port in a storm, darlin'," I drawl. "But right now, there ain't no storm. Piss off."

Letting out a little growl like a pissed-off alley cat, Ginger spins on her high heels and stalks away, steam practically coming out of her ears. She passes the rest of the night climbing all over my other brothers and shooting me dirty looks, trying to get me jealous. But I don't give a fuck — they can have her. Hell, most of them probably have already. Good luck to her, and to them.

As for me, I head over to a group of men clustered around two Ironwood brothers engaged in a drunken wrestling match. It's fight night at the clubhouse, and this is as good a distraction as anything else. I spend the next few hours trading shots with the men, placing bets on who's gonna win the next fight. It's a perfectly decent way to drown my sexual frustrations — trying not to think about the hellhound tattoo with a heart-shaped pupil on my torso, and the golden-haired Mystery Girl with flashing blue eyes who put it there.

13

BULLET

The next morning, I come to on a raggedy-ass couch with springs sticking into my back. I don't remember getting here, and judging from how I feel, I've had a lot more booze than I have sleep. Around me, other Lords are waking up. Some of them are in better shape than me, some worse.

"Jesus fuck," I complain to an Ironwood brother named Rogue. "You assholes need to spend some money on some new furniture."

He grunts in agreement and chuckles. "That's what the

booze is for, brother. You drink enough, your head hurts worse than your back in the morning."

"Ain't that the truth." I wince as I sit up. "I don't know if there's that much whiskey in the world."

The club girls who are still around are busy cleaning up and making us breakfast. Normally, I'd grab myself a red beer — my hair of the dog of choice after a night of drinking — but the run this morning has me taking a more sober approach. I slowly wake up with a cup of black coffee, sitting outside as the morning warms into what promises to be a hot and sticky motherfucker of a day. My dreams are blurry, but I remember Six was in some of them. I'm trying to remember what happened when Angel comes outside and sits down beside me.

"We'll be heading out pretty soon," he grunts. "We got a few hours' drive ahead of us to get to the meet-up."

I grunt back. "I'll be ready."

"You good?" Angel asks. "You've been uncharacteristically quiet since we got here. 'Course," he chuckles. "I shouldn't be looking a gift horse in the mouth."

I snort. "Yeah. I'm good. Just... this run kinda interrupted something I was in the middle of last night."

"In the middle of, or inside of?" Angel smirks.

I laugh. "Fixin' to be inside of."

Angel gives a single nod. "Huh. I saw you brushing off that redhead last night. I was wondering what that was about. You ain't in the habit of turning that shit down, brother."

"Not all tail is created equal, I guess," I mutter.

Angel chuckles. "Don't I know it. Well, don't let yourself get distracted today. This should be a routine run, but you never know."

"Don't worry, boss. I'm good."

He nods. "Okay, then." Standing, he claps me on the back. "I'm gonna head back in. Be ready to go in thirty."

Four hours down, and another four hours back. Everything

goes as planned, with no problems. We meet with our contacts, load up the gun shipment, and arrive back to Ironwood around early dinnertime. When we get back, the Lords are in the kind of good mood that comes from a successful run. I can tell there's another epic party brewing to rival last night's. But instead of looking forward to it, I'm feeling antsy.

Angel is inside the clubhouse with Axel and their two VPs, Beast and Rourke, bottles of beer in hand. I go over and pull him aside.

"Hey, I think I'm gonna head back to Tanner Springs, if you don't need me anymore tonight."

Angel cuts me a look. "You going back to take care of unfinished business?" I nod. "All right, then. See you back there. Don't forget we got church tomorrow."

I lift my chin at him and slip out, before I can get any grief from the other brothers. An hour and a half later, I cross the city limits into Tanner Springs. It's only then that I realize Six might already have plans for tonight. *Well, fuck it. She's gonna change 'em.*

I pull out my phone while I'm gassing up my bike and send her a text.

Back in town. U around?

A few seconds later I get a reply:

Out with Hannah at Lions Tap. Come by

"I DIDN'T THINK I was going to hear from you," Six says calmly as I slide into the booth next to her. Across the table, Hannah greets me with a nod and a sly look from underneath her shelf of fire-engine-red bangs.

"Didn't know how long I was gonna be busy." I signal to Zeb at the bar to get me a beer. "Just got back into town. Haven't even stopped at home yet."

"I'm flattered."

"Hope I'm not crashing your party," I smirk, looking from Six to Hannah.

Hannah sighs loudly and rolls her eyes. "Hardly. You're all Six has been talking about since we got here anyw... *ouch*! Bitch!" She scowls at Six, who I'm guessing just kicked her under the table.

"Is that right?" I cut my gaze to Six. Her face is flaming as she glares back at Hannah.

"Oh, please, Hannah is exaggerating," she insists.

"Like hell I am!" Hannah chortles, shaking her head. She tips back her bottle of beer and drains it just as Zeb appears with mine. "You know what, I'm gonna leave you two to it. I was just a placeholder until you got back anyway, Bullet." She nods at me. "I'd tell you to keep her out of trouble, but I'm not sure you're capable of that."

"She's safe with me."

Hannah snorts good-naturedly. "Right. I'll see you at Rebel Ink, girl." She tilts her head at both of us. "I'd tell you to have a good night, but I think you already got that covered."

I watch as Hannah waves goodbye to the staff and exits the bar, braided plait of scarlet hair swinging between shoulder blades. "I've always liked that girl," I remark with a chuckle. "She knows what's up."

"She's a blabbermouth," Six mutters into her beer.

"So, you've been talking about me, eh?" I tease. "What about, exactly?"

"None of your business." She's clearly uncomfortable, which just makes me want to push her more.

"Maybe... you were telling her about how loud I make you scream when you come?" I let my voice go low and deep, sliding closer to her so she's the only one who can hear me. "Or about how wet your pussy gets when you think about me? Is that what you were talking about, Mystery Girl?" I lean forward and slide my hand between her legs. Her thighs tense, and even with the noise of the bar, I can hear her breath hitch in her throat.

"Stop it..." she pleads in a strangled tone, but her heart's not in it.

"Stop what, baby girl?" With one finger, I lightly graze the fabric of her jeans, just where it covers her clit. Six stifles a moan. "You sure you really want me to stop? Cuz I dunno... it sure doesn't sound like you do."

"Bullet..." she whispers. Her back arches, her breasts straining forward in spite of her best efforts not to show the effect I'm having on her. My cock stiffens as I realize I can feel her getting wet through her jeans. Now it's my turn to stifle a groan.

"You've missed me," I state. She gives me a quick nod, not daring to look me in the eyes. I graze my nail across the fabric above her clit again. She sucks in a breath, her thighs clamping around my hand.

"Babe, I think we need to get out of here. Finish that drink and let's go," I command.

Six doesn't argue with me at all, just raises her beer to her lips with an unsteady hand and downs it. She reaches into the booth and grabs that oversized jacket of hers. Then I'm out of my seat, cock throbbing. I throw a couple bills down on the table. A minute later, we're outside, and she's climbing on the back of my bike.

Neither one of us talks. Our bodies are saying everything that's important. She squirms against me, her hips rocking slightly forward. The way she's moving against me, I'm pretty sure the vibrations from the engine against her clit are driving her crazy. Sure enough, her breasts begin to rise and fall more quickly against my back as I drive. I can feel her trembling with need as she holds onto my waist, but the fact is, she ain't the only one. I'm about to bust out of my skin. I'm hard as a fucking rock and can barely concentrate on steering the bike. It takes everything I've got in me not to just pull over on the side of the road and take her up against my bike. But I want her long, and slow, and all night long. So I tell my dick to calm the fuck down and work on getting us to her place in one piece.

Thank fuck, when we get to her apartment building there's a parking spot about half a block down, in a dark spot between two pools of light from the street lamps. I roll to a stop and cut the engine, then wait for her to hop off the bike. She pulls off the helmet and hands it to me, her eyes huge and dark in her face. She's still breathing fast and hard, her plump lips parted in anticipation.

"Fuck," I groan. "Feels like I've been gone a month."

My mouth comes down on hers, my hands dropping to her ass. I pull her against me, roughly. When she feels the hardness of my erection against her, she moans loudly into my mouth.

"I don't want to talk anymore," she whispers. "Take me upstairs."

I can't resist one more taste of her before we break apart. My lips leave hers, and travel lower, to trace the curve of her chin, then down to her neck. Her skin is soft, sweet like a velvety peach. My cock thickens painfully as I imagine tasting the sweet fruit between her legs, licking the honey from her folds as she cries out in pleasure. *Fuck.* I can't stand anymore. I have to get this girl inside.

I turn her around and place my hand on the small of her back, guiding her up the sidewalk toward the front door of her apartment building. I wait impatiently for her to fit her key into the front lock. My mind is swimming in desire, so dizzy and drunk with the need to have her that it takes me a minute to register what she's saying.

"What?" I ask through the fog of testosterone.

"The door's not locked." She pushes it open with one hand, frowning. "I thought it always locked automatically."

"Fascinating," I rumble. "But that ain't getting us to your apartment any quicker, babe."

She looks up and gives me a breathy laugh. "Sorry," she mumbles, sucking her lower lip between her teeth.

"Fuck, that mouth of yours," I growl. "You do that just to torture me, don't you?"

"Do what?" Wickedly, she lets go of the lip. Deliberately, slowly, she slides her tongue over it.

"You're gonna pay for that, little girl," I warn.

She flashes me a saucy smirk. "I hope so. Over... and over... and over..."

"Oh, Jesus..." I groan, my cock so hard it hurts.

I can't wait to bury my face in her wet, waiting pussy as I watch her ass wiggle in front of me on the way up to her place. I'm so absorbed in the sight, imagining just how I'm gonna strip those tight little jeans off her, that when she stops dead in her tracks I almost run smack into her.

Six gasps, one hand going to her throat. "Oh my God..."

I come around to the side of her, not registering what's happening. "What?"

All color has drained from her face. Wordlessly, she points in front of her. I follow the direction of her arm to see that the door to her place has been kicked in.

"Motherfucker," I fume. "Looks like you've been robbed."

Instantly, I'm on high alert, all thought of sex immediately on the back burner. "Look, it's okay. I got you. We'll check to see what they took, and then call your landlord. You probably ain't the only one who got hit, since they went to the trouble to force the front door. Maybe someone saw something. Hell, maybe someone else got some video foot..."

But Six is shaking her head. She looks like she's seen a ghost. "It's not a robbery," she whispers.

"What? How do you know?"

"Because I know who did this."

"How? Are you sure?"

She nods. I watch as she wearily leans against the wall next to the doorway. She squeezes her eyes shut. "Bullet, I'm sorry. I can't do this."

"Don't worry, darlin'," I answer. "We'll get this taken care of. Like I said, we'll figure out what all they took, if anything. You can decide whether you wanna call the cops, or whether you want the MC to take care of it. You can stay at my place tonight, and tomorrow..."

"No," she cuts me off. Six shakes her head almost violently, looking miserable. "I mean, I have to leave town."

I frown. "What? The fuck are you talking about?"

"I have to leave town. Now. I'm sorry." Her voice breaks.

First, I'm confused. Then, suddenly, I'm angry as fuck. Because I don't know what's going on, but it's clear there is a bunch of shit she is not telling me. And goddamn it, I'm about to find out.

"No. You are not going anywhere. Fuck that, Six." I kick at the half-open door with the toe of my boot. Then I reach for Six's hand and lead her inside. "First, you are gonna tell me what the fuck is going on. And then, we're gonna handle it. Together."

SIX

B ullet is *furious*.
I can't figure out if he's mad at *me*, or mad at the situation, or what. But he's demanding an explanation. And I'm pretty sure there's no way I'm going to get out of giving him one this time.

Tiredly, I follow him inside the bashed-in door of my apartment. Turning on the light, I pull off my old leather jacket and hang it on the hook by the door, suppressing a bitter sigh as I think about where it came from.

I go over to the couch and flop down on it. It barely registers that my place has been tossed. That's the least of my worries right now.

"It was my ex," I murmur, staring down sadly at the rug I love so much. "He's found me."

Bullet's expression turns to stone as he takes in my words. For a few seconds he says nothing. My mind is already starting to mentally pack up. *My suitcases are in the storage locker downstairs. I don't have time to go buy rope to tie the rug to the top of my car, so I'll have to leave it after all. I have enough money in my bank account for maybe two full tanks of gas and...*

"Six."

I look up, befuddled, to see that Bullet has sat down on the couch next to me. His cold, angry eyes bore into mine. "Who the fuck is your ex? And what does that mean, he's found you?"

I let out the breath I don't even realize I've been holding.

"It means exactly that," I sigh. "I thought maybe in Tanner Springs, I'd done a good enough job of disappearing that Flash wouldn't find me for a while." My tone sounds robotic, detached, to hide the fear underneath my words. "I got stupid and stayed too long." I shrug. "I should have known better. So... it's time to go. Before he comes back."

"And does what?" Bullet growls insistently.

My shoulders move up and down again. My blood is rushing in my ears, so when I start talking again, my voice sounds far away. "Tries to hurt me, I guess. Honestly, I don't know why he's so obsessed with me. I thought when I broke it off, he'd just let it go. Or at least get over it eventually. But I don't think that's going to happen until he makes me pay."

"Goddamnit, Six, pay for *what?*" Bullet's eyes are ablaze.

"Breaking up with him in the first place."

I lean back against the sofa cushions and close my eyes. I feel so exhausted all of a sudden. "I never thought he'd be such a psycho. I just thought he was a run of the mill lying, cheating piece of shit. But when I told him we were finished, he wouldn't take no for an answer. He was calling me all the time, telling me it wasn't over, that he needed to see me. I got kind of freaked out by it, to tell you the truth. I was working at a shitty job I hated, and the lease was almost up on my apartment... so I just up and left town." I stare down at a faint coffee ring on the surface of the table in front of me. "And it seems like I've been leaving towns ever since."

Bullet doesn't say anything, seeming to sense I'm not finished. I suppress a shudder at the memories that start flooding in. "I figured that would be the end of it, but instead, he went nuts. He started calling and texting me, demanding to know where I was. When I wouldn't tell him, he'd try to worm it out of my friends, giving them the excuse that he needed to get something from me." I bite the inside of my cheek, remembering. "Thankfully for me, my friends always hated Flash, so they weren't about to tell him anything. And because I didn't want to put them at any risk, I stopped telling them anything about where I was or what I was doing. I cut them off, to protect me and them."

Not for the first time, a wave of odd gratitude floods me that Flash never met my mom, or even knew her name. When I started seeing him, I was in a period of being really angry with her. So I told him she was dead. Since she hardly ever called me or wanted to see me, it was a pretty easy lie to get away with. I can't help but be relieved at how that simple twist of fate has probably stopped Flash from tracking her down to get to me.

"The last time he cornered me was in Chicago," I continue. "He attacked me in public. Tried to rip my clothes off right in the middle of a freaking crowd outside a club." I tear my eyes from the coffee table to look at Bullet. "You know what they say about how in a crowd, no one will step forward to help you? Well, it's true." I let out a bitter laugh. "No one even lifted a finger. It was like we were some sort of street performers, and they were the audience. I finally managed to kick him hard enough that he let go for a second, and was able to pull away from him. At that point, some of the people who had been watching finally seemed to realize he was actually trying to hurt me. Some guys grabbed him and roughed him up, and I was able to get away. I left everything I had in my apartment, and just drove out of town right then and there."

"Fuck," Bullet hisses.

I shake my head again, angry at myself for being lulled into staying so long in one place. "I knew he'd find me again. Deep down, I knew it. He always does." I put my palms on the cushions on either side of me, preparing to stand. "So, I have to leave, Bullet. I'm sorry," I say softly. "I really sort of liked the direction it seemed like this was going."

Bullet's jaw is tight, but his eyes are unexpectedly tender. "Six. Come on. How can you live like this?"

Defensiveness rises up inside me. "It's better than not living at all," I retort. "Or giving myself up to Flash."

Something seems to click in his brain. "Is this why you go by Six?"

Suddenly, I want to tell him. I want to give him something of me. Something *real*. To remember me by.

"Yes." I swallow, and then make myself go on. "My name is Stacia Edison. Six is... well, it's how many different places I've been since going on the run." I smile tremulously. "It's simple. Something I can remember without too much effort. Plus, it has the added benefit of being androgynous. Six could be a girl or a guy. I guess I figure a name like that gives me one more layer of protection. Small as it is."

Bullet's laugh is brittle. "So, did you used to go by Five before this?" When I nod, he shakes his head. "I don't know if that's idiotic or genius."

In spite of everything, that makes me chuckle. "Let's go with somewhere in between."

"So..." he continues, his brow furrowing. "I can't believe I'm suggesting this, but have you ever thought about calling the cops on this piece of shit?"

I blow out a breath. "No. Let's just say I have my reasons for not doing that." I'm pretty sure my record in juvie won't do much to make the police believe my story. And the last thing I want is that kind of scrutiny from the law, when I'm doing my best to stay under the radar.

Thankfully, Bullet doesn't probe. But what he says next is a complete surprise.

"Six. Stacia." The words come out husky, and I shiver a little to hear him say my real name. He reaches out and puts a finger under my chin, lifting it until my eyes meet his. "You're done running."

"But I can't st..."

"You're done. This ends here." His words are final. Resolute. "I'm gonna make this guy go away." Bullet's dark orbs bore into mine. "Do you believe me? Do you trust me?"

I want to. *God,* I want to.

For the first time in years, I let myself imagine for a moment what life would be like if I *could* stop running. If I could stop looking over my shoulder all the time.

The relief that floods through me — even though it's only a specter, a *what-if* — is so sharp that tears spring to my eyes.

I want to believe Bullet that this could all be over. Forever.

So, I whisper, "Yes."

Even though I don't know if it's true.

When Bullet kisses me, his lips are hard, demanding. But when he pulls back to look at me, his gaze is softer than I've ever seen it.

"Come on," he says, standing and reaching down to pull me up with him. "You're gonna stay at my place for a few days. No arguing," he barks when I open my mouth to interrupt him. "Tomorrow, I'm gonna talk to the club. The Lords are gonna take down your ex, once and for all. Don't worry,

Six. You're not gonna have to see this fuckin' weasel ever again."

Bullet gives me a few minutes to pack a small bag with toiletries, a change of clothes, and my laptop, which thankfully is still on my nightstand where I left it. I fret about not being able to bring more, but he promises me we can come back tomorrow or the next day.

Finally, when I'm ready, he holds his large, strong hand out to me, and I take it.

Something seems to shift in the air between us as I allow Bullet to lead me out of my apartment. With a mixture of relief and apprehension, I realize I've confided more in Bullet than I have to anyone since I first started running. I've told him things that no one else knows. Not even Hannah. For better or worse, I've decided to I've put my trust in him.

The last time I trusted a man, I ended up having to give up everything I knew, just to save myself.

And only time will tell if I've just made yet another huge mistake.

15

BULLET

Once we're out of Six's apartment, I don't call her by her real name again. She seemed to sort of flinch when I said it — like it's a door to her past life that she'd prefer to keep closed, at least for now.

But the sound of it rolls over and over in my mind. Stacia. It's a secret. A confidence. A sign that I've broken through one of the walls that she's built so high around herself.

I know Six would never have asked me for help with the piece of shit who's stalking her. Hell, she was willing to pack up and leave town before she'd let anyone else in. This girl is used to going it alone. If I hadn't been with her when she got home tonight, she would have been gone without a trace, and I'd never have seen her again.

The thought hits me like a shot to the gut, to know how close I came to losing her.

It's kind of fucked up to be worrying about losing some chick I hardly know.

Except, Six isn't just some chick.

There's something about this girl. And it's more than the fact she's a hot piece of ass. It's true, up until tonight I knew next to nothing about her.

But I want to know more. A lot more.

And the best way to get there is to make sure she doesn't get freaked out and leave town. Because one thing I do know after tonight is that this girl has gotten damn good at disappearing. And I sure as shit don't want her disappearing on me now.

When we get to my place, she doesn't talk much. I can tell she's a little freaked out at the idea of staying with me. She hesitates in the doorway, like she doesn't want to intrude. And even though I tell her to make herself at home, she looks like she's trying to make herself as small as possible.

Six deposits her backpack on the floor next to one corner of the couch. She pulls off her jacket and sets it down, too. Her expression is pinched, and it's pretty obvious that tonight has taken a toll on her. "I, um... could I just get a blanket for the couch?" she asks hesitantly. "I'm sort of tired. If you don't mind, maybe I'll just go to sleep."

In spite of myself, I roar with laughter, so loud it startles her. "What the fuck, Six? You're not sleeping on my couch. Come on," I growl, picking up her backpack. "The bed's big enough for two."

"Are you sure?" she swallows, reddening. "I mean... you don't have to..."

"Don't be dumb," I cut her off. "I'm not having you sleep out here. And I sure as shit ain't sleeping on the couch, either."

Then I see the troubled look on her face and try to sound more gentle. "Come on, Six. You said you're tired. Don't overthink this."

I don't wait for an answer. I figure she'll follow me since I have her stuff. Turns out, I'm right. When I get to my bedroom, I toss her backpack on the mattress and turn around. She's standing in the doorway again, looking like she's waiting for an invitation. I cock my head at her, and she seems to realize what she's doing.

"Sorry," she murmurs, and steps through the door.

"It's not much. And I wasn't expecting visitors," I rumble, nodding toward the unmade king-size bed. At least I washed the sheets not too long ago.

"It's great." She gives me a tiny smile. "Thank you, Bullet."

Six bends over and rummages in her backpack, pulling out a toothbrush and a tube of paste. "I'm gonna go brush my teeth."

"Bathroom's through there," I say, pointing.

"Thanks," she nods. She takes a step toward the hallway, and then stops. "Oh!"

"What is it?"

"I, um..." She purses her lips. "You're gonna laugh at me."

"No, I'm not. What is it?"

She exhales softly. "I forgot to bring something to sleep in."

I burst out laughing again.

Six rolls her eyes. "I *told* you you were gonna laugh at me," she mutters.

I clear my throat and try to stop. "Look, darlin', I'm sorry, but if you don't want me to laugh, don't say such stupid shit. Do I have to remind you where my tongue's been?"

"Could you not... say that quite so crudely?"

"Oh, darlin', that ain't crude. Crude would be..."

"*Stop! Lalalalalalalala!*" Six cringes and claps her hands over her ears.

"Okay, okay!" I snicker. "But enough with the 'I don't have a flannel nightie that buttons up to my chin' Victorian-ass bullshit."

Six mumbles something I don't catch, flips me off, and makes a break for the bathroom. Chuckling, I go out into the living room to give her some space. While I'm out there, I get a call from Hale about some club business, so I step outside to take it. By the time I get back inside about ten minutes later, the bathroom's empty. I go into the bedroom to see how Six is doing.

She's lying in bed, the covers pulled up around her. Fast asleep.

I snort and shake my head as I kick off my boots and strip off my clothes. To say tonight did not go according to plan would be the understatement of the damn year.

Still, even though I was really looking forward to getting back between those thighs of hers, there's something to be said about seeing her there, in my bed, looking about as relaxed as I've ever seen her.

I push back the covers and get in beside her, trying to ignore the hard-on I've been dealing with since before she went into the bathroom. As if on cue, Six sighs deeply and turns toward me, curling her body into the space between my arm and my side. I stifle a groan as my cock grows harder. Jesus Christ, going to sleep next to her tonight is gonna be damn near impossible.

This is a first, for sure. In fact, it's a whole night of firsts.

I should be pissed. Not at her, but at myself. The rational part of my brain is telling me I'm a goddamn idiot for bringing a woman I barely know to stay at my house, for Christ knows how long.

I don't bring women home. Not even to fuck. And sure as hell not to stay.

Then again, I've never wanted to before now.

And shit, there's no way I could have left Six alone in her apartment after her piece of shit ex broke in. I wasn't about to bring her to a hotel, either. Especially because I'm sure she would have skipped town during the night, even if I managed to get her to promise me she wouldn't. The only way I can keep her here in Tanner Springs is if I keep an eye on her. She might think she's safer leaving, but I know that ain't true.

If I'm gonna protect her, I need to keep her close.

But that's not the only reason I want her here. Much as I hate to admit it.

I want her here for *me*. Because I don't want to lose her. Not like this.

I don't know where this shit is going with me and Six. But I plan to find out. And no dickhead ex-boyfriend with boundary problems is gonna fuck with that.

THE NEXT MORNING, Six wakes up just as I'm getting up to go take a shower. Apparently, a decent night's sleep has put her in a good mood, because the first thing she does is cut me a sly glance as I'm standing up from the bed.

"Is that for me?" She gives me a wicked look.

I glance down at my dick, which is at half-staff.

"It sure as hell can be." My voice is thick. "You wanna join me in the shower?"

Six sucks in a breath.

"That's one heck of an invitation," she murmurs. "Not sure I can resist it."

My cock snaps to full attention.

"Shower. Thirty seconds," I say, turning away.

By the time I enter the bathroom, I'm painfully hard, my erection throbbing a low, steady beat as I turn on the shower head. I push open the fiberglass door and step inside, hearing Six's soft steps padding in behind me as I do.

"Sorry I passed out last night," she breathes against my back as she wraps her arms around me from behind. "I guess I was more tired than I thought."

"Stress will do that to you." I turn around and reach for her. She's standing under the shower spray, her body already glistening and wet. Rivulets of water slide between her breasts, down her stomach to her pussy. My cock throbs harder. "You know it was fucking torture lying next to you last night."

"Really?" Her lips part, her dark-pupilled gaze locking on mine. Want is written all over her face.

"Really." My hands slide over her body, my thumb grazing an already hardening nipple. Her eyes half-close in a shudder. Jesus fuck, she's sexy. "You drive me fucking crazy, Six. I've never wanted a woman as much as I want you."

I can't believe I just told her that, but I don't fucking care. It's the truth. Before I can think to take the words back, my mouth is on hers. I kiss her long and hard, my mouth devouring hers before gliding over her wet skin, down to her neck. Her moan is low and keening, telling me she needs this as much as I do without her having to say a word.

"Oh, fuck, baby," I groan. I reach down and cup her ass, then pull her up and brace her against the wall. I want to take it slow and make this last, but I'm too turned on and the way she's writhing her hips against me tells me she needs it now, fast and hard. Her whimpers turn to soft cries as she wraps her legs around my waist and I angle myself up so the head of my cock is nestled against the wet heat of her pussy. "Need to be inside you," I grunt.

"Yes, Bullet," she pants, as I cover my mouth with hers again. Rocking my hips, I push myself inside her and she moans into my mouth, clinging to me as I begin to thrust. The angle of my cock is brushing against her clit just right, I can tell by the way she meets me thrust for thrust, and soon the entire world drops away and it's just us, our bodies taking and giving, me burying myself inside her deeper with every stroke, until suddenly she tenses in my arms. Her pussy begins to contract around me as Six whispers my name like a prayer. Seconds later, my balls begin to tighten, and with a final thrust I drive deep inside her and find my own release.

Half an hour later, I'm guessing we've probably used up ninety percent of the water in Tanner Springs.

"Being clean never felt so dirty," Six quips as I toss her a towel. "Is this how you're gonna wake me up every morning that I'm here?"

"I guess you're gonna have to find out," I wink back at her.

But even though my tone is joking, I gotta admit I like the sound of that.

What would it be like to wake her up every morning... *forever*?

Huh.

I INSTRUCT Six to call in sick to work and stay locked in at my place. She starts to protest, but I manage to convince her by promising her it's just for one day.

"Do this for me, Six," I insist. "You trust me, right?"

My chest tightens with emotion when she doesn't even hesitate. "Yes. Of course I do."

"Okay, then. Sit tight. I promise I've got it covered. Just do this for me today, so I don't have to worry about you while I'm getting shit together. Promise?"

"I promise."

After kissing her goodbye, I drive to the clubhouse to find Angel. I tell him as much as I know about Six's douchebag ex-boyfriend, and ask my prez for a couple of men to keep an eye on her apartment.

Angel agrees immediately. "Whatever you need, brother, you let me know. Who do you want?"

I pause. "Striker and Tank. That oughta be enough for now."

He nods. "You got it."

I go round up the men and tell them what I have in mind. I ask Striker and Tank to switch off standing watch outside her apartment building for a day or two, and tell them to get in touch with me if they see anything suspicious or even out of the ordinary. I decide I'm going to follow Six myself, including when she's at work, so I know she's always safe.

I'm coming out of Angel's office when I run into Tweak. "Hey, I got some more intel on Edge for you," he tells me. "Courtesy of Oz's man Rodrigo."

"No time for that now," I tell him. "Hang onto it. Right now I got something else I need to deal with." I pause as a thought occurs to me. "Matter of fact, I might need your assistance on that."

Tweak looks at me in surprise. "You sure?"

"Positive. Ellis will keep for a few more days. Ask Oz to keep eyes on him so he doesn't disappear."

Tweak nods, frowning. "Okay, got it."

I don't blame him for wondering what the fuck is up with me. He doesn't know everything about why I'm so hell bent on finding my stepdad, but he does know Ellis is the reason I spent two years in prison. And he knows this is the revenge I've been seeking for years. Now, it's right here on my doorstep, so close I can practically touch it. I should be chomping at the bit.

But Ellis will have to wait.

I wasn't able to save my mom from him.

But I can sure as hell save Six now.

And nothing is going to stop me from doing that.

When I go back to my place to tell Six about the surveillance I've set up, I ask her to give me a description of the piece of shit she calls Flash. She tells me his actual name is Sam Randall. She describes him as having the looks of a frat boy, with light blond hair in a floppy nineties cut.

"He's about your height," she continues, crossing her arms and squinting at me. "But a lot less muscular. And fewer tattoos."

"Got any pictures of him?"

"No... Well, wait."

Six uncrosses her legs and gets up off the couch. Padding into the bedroom, she returns a few seconds later with her laptop. She pulls it open and sits back down. I watch as she peers at the screen, types in a website, then spends a couple of minutes clicking through some screens and typing some more.

"There," she finally says, turning the computer to me.

I lean forward and take a look. It's what appears to be a governmental records website. A picture of an asshole-looking blond guy stares back at me. Underneath it, a name, date of birth, and a bunch of other details show on the screen.

"'Sam Randall'," I read, and then calculate his age from the birthdate listed there. "No middle name. Thirty-one years old. What the fuck is this, Six?" I ask. "Did you hack into some cop website?"

"Nah," she laughs. "No hacking necessary. Finding this stuff is nothing that complicated. It's easy to find, as long as you know where to look. But..." she hesitates. "If you need me to find any less publicly available info on Flash, I can do that, too."

"What else can you do?" I ask, raising a brow.

"Well," she continues slowly. "I can create enough documentation to allow me to get ID cards under different names, with enough backup in the system to satisfy anyone doing a background check."

"Holy shit," I marvel. "I'll have to introduce you to Tweak."

"Who?"

"Our MC's resident hacker and all-around computer genius." I chuckle. "Then again, if I do introduce you to him, he's likely to propose to you on the spot."

16

BULLET

"Above all," I tell Six, "just act normal. Like no one's following you. But I'll be there all the time. You're not in any danger. Anything happens with this piece of shit — if he gets anywhere near you — I'll be on him like white on rice."

At first, Six continues to protest, saying she doesn't want to put me or the MC out by having us watch her. But in the end, I think the prospect of finally being able to stop running from her ex makes her stop arguing.

Nothing happens for two days. Six goes back to work, and everything returns to normal, except that she continues to stay at my place. Having her in my bed every night is better than I could have imagined. I learn her body — every curve, every place that makes her shiver, every caress that makes her gasp and moan my name. She falls asleep in my arms every night, and I wake her up with my tongue between her legs every morning.

I don't talk at all about what's happening between us, or the future. She doesn't bring it up, either. This ain't the time for touchy-feely conversation. It's easier — and less complicated — just to focus on the task at hand: bringing down this douchebag who calls himself Flash.

There's no activity at her apartment building, so I call off Tank and Striker and tell them I'll be in touch if I need backup.

On the third day, Six runs out of clean clothes, so she texts me from Rebel Ink saying she wants to go back to her apartment after her shift to grab some stuff.

I get there before her, and let myself in the back door of the building with the duplicate keys she's given me. I don't think Douchebag Flash is smart enough to have noticed the Lords have been keeping an eye on the building — but just in case, I drive over in a cage and leave my cut in the trunk. Once I'm there, I do a quick eyeball perimeter check and don't see anything unusual. Then I go inside and clear Six's apartment.

Except for her sparse mishmash of furniture, it's empty and silent. It doesn't look like anyone's been in here since the night of the break-in. But that doesn't mean shit. I'm not about to leave her alone in this place for even one second. I go into the bedroom and climb into Six's small closet, cracking the door just an inch. Then I pull myself into a squat behind the clothes to wait.

About fifteen minutes after the end of Six's shift, the key turns in the lock of the recently-repaired door. The light, quick steps tell me it's her. Six knows I'm in here somewhere — I promised her I would be — but I've instructed her not to say a word to me and pretend she's in here alone.

She pads through the living room, picking up an object or two, then comes into the bedroom. I hear a bag being set on the bed, and the sound of a zipper. More light footsteps, then a dresser drawer opening. I stay where I am, still poised for attack. Suddenly, the closet door creaks, and Six's face appears. She starts to reach toward the clothes hanging in front of her, then her body stiffens as she turns and sees me. Her eyes open wide as she starts and suppresses a cry, then flashes me an angry look whose meaning is clear. *You scared me!*

I lift one shoulder and give her a smirk. *Sorry, babe.*

Shaking her head slightly, she pulls something off of a hanger and slips back out again.

I stifle a snort of amusement and start to draw myself back into my crouch. Just then, a thud and a cry out in the hall sends me bolting to my feet. I spring out of the closet, just in time to see Six struggling to fight off a tall, lanky blond guy, who has one arm around her throat and another wrenching her arm behind her back.

With a roar, I launch myself at Flash, ripping him away from Six just as he turns toward me in shock. He reacts quicker than I expect, pulling himself into a crouch and then a roll that gets him away from me. He stumbles up onto his feet and starts to run for the half-open door, reaching it before me, but I'm just close enough to launch myself forward and connect with his back. The momentum propels him into the door itself, slamming it shut as he barrels into it face-first. I grab him by the shirt as he starts to stagger, and swivel him around so he's facing me. His nose is bloodied, probably broken, and his eyes are leaking tears from the pain, but that's not good enough. I pull back and throw the most satisfying fucking punch of my life. It connects squarely with his upper cheek and already fucked-up nose, snapping his head back on his neck, and then he's out, eyes rolling back into their sockets.

I let go of him and his unconscious body slumps to the floor.

For a second, there's silence. Then, a high burble of laughter emerges from Six's throat.

"Well, that didn't take very long," she giggles. Her voice is shaking, probably from the quick jolt of adrenaline her body no longer needs. She looks down at the prone figure of her ex-boyfriend, and the dribble of blood emerging from his mouth. "Thanks for not getting blood on my rug," she quips as her body starts to tremble. "I love that rug."

"Shhh, babe. It's okay. It's over now." I put my arm around Six and hug her tight against me, to stop her from freaking out. To her credit, she manages to calm herself right down, after clinging to me for a minute and taking a some deep breaths to steady herself.

Finally, she lets out a shuddering exhale and detaches herself from me. "What now?" she asks me.

I ask her if she has any rope, and she goes out of the room and brings back a roll of pink duct tape.

"Will this work?"

"Perfect."

I bind Flash's hands and feet, and then we prop him up on the floor with his back against the side of the bed. He doesn't move or stir as the blood continues to trickle from his mouth and nose, staining his shirt.

"Man. How hard did you hit him?" Six marvels.

"Not half as hard as I wanted to." Leaning down, I slap him across the face a couple of times with the back of my hand. He groans, his head lolling to one side.

"Wake the fuck up, Princess," I bark. "It's show time."

Flash pries his eyes open, squinting up at us as he comes to.

He seems to register where he is all at once, because his face goes from confusion to rage in a millisecond.

"What the fuck?" he roars, wrenching at the tape binding his wrists. He tries to lunge toward us.

"Breaking into a lady's apartment is a dick move, Junior." I lift up a boot and plant it in his chest, kicking him backwards. "You really that hard up for pussy?"

"Fuck you," he coughs out, trying to catch his breath.

"Jesus, Flash," Six blurts, reaching for my arm just as I start toward him. "Do you want him to break your jaw? Or worse?"

"Here's the thing, Junior," I begin. As calmly as I can, I detach Six's hand from my bicep and squat down. "You're stalking a woman who's under my protection. You've broken into her place twice now. I saw you trying to hurt her." I stare daggers into his eyes. "You're proving to be a problem. I don't like problems. The way I deal with them is, I remove them. You get me?"

"Why can't you just leave me alone, Flash?" Six cries. "It's not like you were even that into me when we were together. Why can't you just take no for an answer? My God. Please, just move on!"

But instead of answering, this douchebag just opens his bloody mouth and lets out a short, barking laugh.

"Fuck you, Stace," he snarls. "You ain't all that. You weren't even that good in bed. I could have a hundred bitches better than you any day of the week. I don't give a shit about you. What I want is the key!"

Six gapes at him. "What key?"

"The key that was in my goddamn jacket when you stole it, you bitch!"

Six raises her hands in a sweeping gesture. "Flash, what the hell are you talking about? I don't have any damn key! There was no key in your jacket!"

Douchebag's eyes widen in disbelief. "Are you fuckin' serious? Oh, Jesus Christ!" He starts to laugh again. "Are you really so fucking stupid that you took off with it and never even fuckin' knew you had it?"

He continues to howl with helpless laughter. My fists clench as I step toward him, eager to flatten his goddamn nose and shatter the cartilage into useless shards. "Listen, Fuckface," I shout, grabbing him by the collar and hauling him up onto the bed. "We're done having fuckin' social hour. What. Fucking. Key?"

"Take a look if you don't believe me," Flash grins. Blood stains his teeth red, making him look like a skinny demon. "There's a key sewn into that leather jacket Stace stole from me."

Six's eyes meet mine. Mutely, she goes into the bedroom and brings out the oversized jacket she's always wearing.

"That's his?" I growl, a pang of jealousy surprising me.

Flash's eyes widen greedily when he sees it. "There. It should be sewn into the bottom part, by the left pocket."

Six feels around the bottom hem of the jacket. Her fingers stop as they grasp something hard. Silently, she nods at me.

"Give it to me, and I'll leave right now," Flash wheedles.

But I shake my head. "Rip it open," I tell Six. "Let's see it."

Six looks around and then grabs a ball point pen that's sitting on her dresser. She slides it under the thread and rips enough of it out that she's able to work the key out from the hem. Once it's free, she holds it up to show me.

"See?" Flash coaxes. "That's all I want. Just give it to me and you'll never fucking see me again."

"Not so fast, Fuckface," I growl, turning. "You're gonna need to tell us what that key is for first."

I can almost see the calculations he's doing as he works his swelling jaw. He must want that key pretty fuckin' bad, because he starts talking almost immediately. "You're not the only one who's been on the run, Stace," he starts, glancing at her. "You remember Paco and Grimm? The key is ours."

"Oh, *shit*," Six breathes.

"What does that mean?" I demand. Six starts to answer but I cut her off. "I wanna hear this from Fuckface."

Flash ignores the insult. "These guys, Paco and Grimm. Them and me used to do some business together," he says vaguely.

"They're thieves," Six inserts flatly. "Felons. So's Flash, for that matter." She looks at me. "Paco and Grimm are in prison."

"*Were* in prison," Flash corrects.

"Flash pulled a heist with them a few years ago. This was before we met. I didn't know any of this until Flash and I had been together for a while." Six's eyes are full of disgust. "It was a jewel heist. But they got caught. Paco and Grimm took the fall, but Flash managed to escape. They've been in prison for years, but I guess they're out now. Huh, Flash?"

"Yeah," he agrees. "And if it wasn't for you taking off, I woulda been long gone by now. I was waiting to fence the jewels when they weren't so hot." He shoots Six a look of anger. "But you skipped town with my goddamn jacket, and the key to the fucking safe deposit box." Flash's face turns violent as he stares at Six with loathing. But one look from me and he tamps that shit down fast. "I been tracking them through the system. Pac got out last week. Grimm's hearing was yesterday. They'll be coming for me. I gotta get that key, Stace." He tries a pleading look. "I gotta get out of sight. You know what they'll do if they find me."

Six shakes her head. "Jesus, Flash." Her lip curls. "Why the hell couldn't you have just told me?"

"So let me get this straight," I cut in. "You mean to tell me, you were gonna take the key from Six and leave her to face these two thugs without even a warning?"

Flash frowns in confusion. "Six?"

"Babe, we don't know what these guys Paco and Grimm know. They could be coming for you, to see if you know where he is."

Six looks at me, blanching. "Do you really think that's a possibility?" she whispers.

"We can't take any chances. I'm gonna call in the Lords for backup." I grab my phone out of my back pocket. "Meanwhile, we're gonna store your friend here in a warehouse nearby for a bit."

"What?" Flash chokes out. "You can't fucking do that! I gotta get gone!"

"Don't worry, Princess," I growl. "You'll be under guard. No one will be able to hurt your delicate self." He starts to holler and struggle. "Oh for fuck's sake," I mutter. Grabbing the duct tape from the top of the dresser, I pull off a pink strip and tape it over his mouth. Fuckface keeps trying to yell, but now nothing's coming out.

"There. Jesus, that's better, ya fuckin' pansy."

I punch in Angel's number on my phone and wait for him to answer.

"Hello, prez?" I say when he does. "You know that situation I was telling you about? Well, turns out I'm gonna need a few more men."

SIX

Half an hour later, there's a knock at my door. Bullet lets in two men wearing Lords of Carnage cuts. One of them I immediately recognize from the Smiling Skull.

"You remember Tank," he says. "This is Hollis."

"Hey there, darlin'," Tank greets me, one corner of his mouth lifting. "Guess you didn't take our advice about the farts."

"Not the time, asshole," Bullet warns.

Tank gives me a quick wink, and the two men follow Bullet into the bedroom. When Flash sees them come in, he starts trying to yell again through the duct tape over his mouth. Tank, who's the larger of the two, unceremoniously punches him in the jaw, knocking him out cold for the second time tonight.

I almost feel sorry for my ex-boyfriend. Almost.

Tank and Hollis load Flash's unconscious body into a large duffel bag, which Tank tosses over his shoulder like it's a sack of potatoes. "You know where we're takin' him," Tank mutters at Bullet, with a glance at me. "Hollis is gonna guard him overnight. Angel will send someone to take over in the morning."

Bullet nods. "I'll be in touch."

Tank and Hollis leave with the bag. Bullet looks at me. "You ain't staying here tonight." It's not a question. "I don't care that we got Flash. We don't know if anyone's coming for him yet."

"I'm not arguing," I say with a shiver. "This whole thing just got a lot bigger than I thought it was. I don't know Paco and Grimm. They were in prison already when I met Flash. But what I've heard from him about them isn't good."

I'm subdued as we ride back to Bullet's place. He doesn't push me to talk, for which I'm grateful. I'm having trouble digesting everything that's just happened. I want to talk about it, eventually, but I need some time to collect my thoughts.

Once we're back at his house, I go out into his back yard and grab an old plastic lawn chair that's sitting next to the back door. Plopping down on it, I stare out at the trees at the edge of his yard, fingering the key that's now nestled in my jacket pocket, lost in my thoughts.

A few minutes later, Bullet comes out to join me, a couple of bottles of beer in his hand.

"Well," I joke grimly as he hands me one. "At least Flash isn't an unhinged stalker like I thought he was."

"Yeah." He grabs another chair and sits down next to me. "He's just a dumbshit petty thug with a couple of jewel thieves after him."

"I can't believe it," I breathe. "I spent all this time on the run from him, thinking he was crazed with possessive anger because I broke up with him." I take the key out of my pocket and hold it up at eye level. "When if I'd just known he was looking for this," I marvel. "So much trouble for one little key."

"Whatever's in that safe deposit box must be pretty valuable," Bullet observes.

"I gave up my whole life for this key. My whole identity. I've lived a lie for almost three years for this thing."

Suddenly, I have the irrational urge to go find a bridge and fling the damn thing off of it.

"You miss it?" Bullet asks. "Your old life?"

"I'm tired of running," I reply. Then I pause, thinking about his question. "I'm tired of worrying. Of being afraid to get close to anyone. But no, I don't exactly miss my old life, as such. It wasn't all that great, to be honest."

"How come?"

"Well... I told you my dad died when I was a teenager. And I love my mom, but she's had a drinking problem for as long as I can remember. So, uh, I didn't exactly have a lot of great role models growing up. Or a lot of family." I pause. "Flash isn't the first shitty boyfriend I've had. My first one, Jesse, stole cars. I was fifteen. I thought it was true love. I don't know, I pictured us as this sort of Bonnie and Clyde thing. Until he got arrested for grand theft auto. I was in the car with him. I ended up in juvie. I guess I was just lucky it was my first offense, and I was young, and a girl." I look over at Bullet and shake my head ruefully. "I really know how to pick 'em, don't I?"

But Bullet doesn't question it or make fun of me. "Sounds like kind of a lonely life," he remarks instead. "Maybe you just ended up being a target for men who wanted a girl they could take advantage of."

I scoff. "That just makes me an idiot."

"No." His voice comes out unexpectedly harsh. "That just

makes you someone with a big heart. Maybe you've made some mistakes, Six. Everyone has. Shit, you think I'm in an outlaw MC because I'm a fuckin' choir boy? I told you about what brought me here. We both had a rough childhood. What matters now is what you make of it in the rest of your life."

I consider his words. The truth is, I haven't been making *anything* out of my life. There hasn't been time. When you have to be ready to move at a moment's notice, you learn to exist in a kind of holding pattern.

My job at Rebel Ink — and actually learning how to be a tattoo artist — is the closest I've come to making a life that includes plans, or any sense of having a future. And hell, even there I just kind of fell into it by chance. I just happened to meet Hannah one night at a bar when her date stood her up. If she hadn't been by herself and pissed off enough to complain to a stranger — and if I hadn't been a couple drinks in and more willing than usual to exchange female confidences — we never would have started talking. She never would have volunteered that her boss was looking for a receptionist, and encouraged me to apply.

Even that — arguably the only good decision I've made since I skipped out on Flash — wasn't even really my doing.

"That's just it," I say somberly to Bullet. "I haven't been making anything of it. I'm not sure I know how to. I don't really have anything to offer. Other than being reasonably competent at tattoos, I guess."

Bullet fixes me with a hard stare. "Stop that. You know a shitload about computers, don't you? Enough to change your identity over and over without any trouble. How the hell did you learn that?"

I shrug. "Necessity."

"Well, if you can do that, you can do anything you put your mind to."

"Maybe." I yawn. I'm suddenly exhausted by all the events

of the day. And I'm sick of talking about how dumb and pathetic my life choices have been. "Right now, I think I'm gonna put my mind to going to sleep." I glance at him. "Right after I take care of something. Do you have a needle and thread?"

Bullet wrinkles his brow. "Uh... I have a needle. Not sure about thread. Why?"

I pull the key out of my pocket again and dangle it in front of him. "I want to sew this back into the lining of the jacket for now."

Bullet manages to find a needle and some dental floss in a junk drawer. It only takes me a few minutes to sew the key back into the lining. Anyone who looked closely would notice the stitching right away, so it's not exactly invisible. Still, right now I care less about that, and more about not losing this key before we figure out what to do with it.

THE NEXT MORNING, Bullet decides to take me to the place where they're keeping Flash.

"We need to talk to him," he rumbles. "Ask him more about this safe deposit box. Where it is, and exactly what's in it. He ain't gonna tell me, probably, but you might be able to get it out of him."

"I doubt it, but I'll try," I frown.

"Thing is, this place where we're going... it's secret. No one outside of the club knows about it."

"So, what, you're gonna blindfold me?" I joke. Then I see the expression on his face. "Wait, you *are* gonna blindfold me? What the hell, Bullet?"

"It's not a big deal. Just until we get there. It's for your protection."

I roll my eyes. "Whatever."

Bullet doesn't want me hanging on to the back of his bike

with no eyesight, so we take my car. I bitch a bit about him driving instead of me, but I know he's not about to back down. So eventually I just accept it and let it go.

We drive for about half an hour, maybe more, on windy, hilly roads that make my stomach dip and flip since I'm blind. Eventually, the car slows and stops.

"Okay, we're here. You can take that thing off."

I pull off the bandana he's given me and look around. The landscape is nondescript, the building even more so. It's an old ranch style house, with weeds growing all around it. I climb out of the car and follow Bullet toward the front door.

"Hold up for a sec." He taps on the front screen in a series of knocks that must be a code.

We wait. Nothing happens.

Bullet taps again. When no one answers, he frowns at me and reaches into his waistband, drawing out a gun. I freeze, not realizing he was armed.

"Go back out to the car," he murmurs. "Get in and slide down so no one can see you. Lock the doors."

I open my mouth to ask why, but the question dies in my throat. Wordlessly, I nod and slip down off the concrete porch. I get into the car and close the passenger door as quietly as I can.

In the silence of the car, I can hear my labored breathing. My heart is hammering in my chest. All my muscles tense up as I wait for a gunshot or a scream or something, and my mind races as I try to think what I should do next.

But when the sound does come, it's none of those things. It's Bullet's voice.

"Six," he calls.

I heave a giant sigh of relief and slide back up into the seat. I open the car door again and walk toward the house, grinning at him. But the grin freezes on my lips when I see the look on his face.

"Flash is dead," he mutters as I climb the steps.

"What?" I gape up at him, thinking this is some sort of joke, but his eyes are dead serious. "How —?"

"Hollis is dead, too." His jaw sets.

"Oh my God!" I start to go inside, but Bullet bars the entrance.

"No. Don't go in." I try to go around him, but he grabs my arm. "Six. They've both been tortured. There's a lot of blood." He shakes his head once, emphatically. "You don't want to see it. Trust me. Stuff like that, it stays with you a long time."

"Bullet," I whisper, my legs weakening under me. He catches me by the shoulders and leads me back away from the house to the car.

"I know." He pulls open the passenger door, nodding at me to get in. "We have to get you out of here, Six. We're leaving town. I'm taking you to someplace safe."

I can only listen to his words through the muddiness of my brain and try to arrange them in a way that makes sense. "Will you be with me?"

"I'm not leaving you," he says fiercely. "I promise. Now give me a minute. I gotta call the Lords. Tell them we got trouble."

18

BULLET

Six is white as a sheet as I peel away from the house where Flash and Hollis's bodies lie in their own respective pools of blood. I'm glad as shit she didn't see any of that. I know she's had a rough life, but I can tell just by how basically sweet and innocent she is that she's never seen a dead body. Especially one that's been tortured like those two were.

That shit comes back to torture you in your sleep. I don't want her to have to live with those visions in her head.

She's afraid but quiet as I race down the highway, yelling into my phone to Angel. "Two bodies. Hollis is one of them. The other is Six's ex. The state of the bodies suggests they were tortured for information. Has to be the guys he was running from. They're looking for a key to a safe deposit box with a cache of stolen jewelry and maybe some other shit."

Angel swears. "Fuck. Hollis's girlfriend is gonna lose it. I'll have Brooke and a couple of the other old ladies go break the news. How the fuck did they find the house?"

"No clue. No telling where they are now, either. I'm taking Six to Connegut."

"I'll send you some backup."

"Thanks. I'll be in touch."

I hang up and turn to Six. "We'll be good as soon as we get to where we're going. My prez is sending men to meet us." I reach over and take one of her hands in mine. It's cold. "Don't worry."

"What's Connegut?" she asks, her voice so soft I can barely hear her.

"It's what we call one of our safe houses. It's on the Connegut River."

"'Safe'," she repeats, a little sharply. "Like the place you were holding Flash?"

Point taken. "No." I shake my head. "It's isolated. Protected." I glance at Six and give her hand a squeeze. "No one is going to hurt you," I say fiercely. "I'll end anyone who tries to lay a hand on you. You trust me?"

Six hesitates, then dips her head. "Yes."

We drive mostly in silence, but the tension in the car is thick enough to cut with a knife. I'm trying to figure out how these fucking goons found where we were holding Flash. They must have followed us. Which has me glancing in my rear view mirror every couple of miles or so, even though there's almost no one on the road.

"We'll have backup to the safe house," I repeat, breaking the silence. "It won't be just me there. They won't get anywhere near you."

"Okay."

Six's voice is flat. I don't know if she believes me.

"You scared, babe?"

She's quiet. Then: "A little. But in a way, this is almost a relief." She blows out a breath. "I've been running for so long from something I didn't even understand. This is a lot scarier in some respects, but at least one way or another, it'll be over soon."

"Not one way or another," I growl. "This ends with them dead."

Six swallows. "Bullet..."

"Yeah."

"You shouldn't be putting your club in danger for me. Breaking the law for me."

I snort. "The law? Fuck the law. We go by our own codes, babe. And we protect our own."

"But that's just it," she insists stubbornly. "I'm *not* one of your own. None of you has any obligation to protect me."

"Like hell you're not." My voice comes out louder, angrier than I intended. Six flinches, and I force myself to calm down. "You're with me. That's good enough for the Lords. So, shut up and let me protect you."

For the first time, a little humor slips through in her voice. "Really? That's a little caveman, don't you think?"

I roll my eyes and pretend to be irritated. "So sorry, milady. I didn't mean to offend your delicate fuckin' sensibilities. Would you be so kind as to allow me to defend your honor?"

Six snickers. "You suck as Sir Lancelot."

"Good. Wasn't that chick he was defending married, anyway? I don't do married chicks. Too much goddamn work to get laid."

"You're a pig," Six laughs.

"I'm a pig because I don't chase married chicks?"

"No, because all you think about is sex. Would you be protecting me if we hadn't —" Six stops talking abruptly.

"What?"

"Uh-oh," she hisses. "Look behind us."

I'm about to ask her what she means, but a check of my mirror tells me instantly. Two cars have appeared over the hill behind us. They're driving two abreast, and gaining on us quickly.

"Shit." I punch the accelerator with my foot, and Six's engine groans in protest before starting the process of speeding up. This compact ain't the car I would have chosen for a high-speed chase, but I don't have much of a choice right now. I fly over the next hill, and suddenly my foot leaves the accelerator and slams on the brakes, lurching us forward in our seats.

There's a van at two-hundred feet ahead of us, blocking both lanes. Ditches on either side mean I can't chance driving off the road.

We're fucked.

I slow the car, scanning the scene quickly to assess our situation. There's at least two people in each of the vehicles. We're outnumbered three to one. I could pull out my piece and start shooting, but neither Six or I would make it out of that alive. Instead, I keep it hidden in my waistband and hope no one takes it off me before I have a chance to use it.

"Get the fuck outta the car!" one of the men yells, waving a gun at us and miming taking aim. Six flinches, but looks at me for direction. I nod once.

"Stay alert," I murmur. "We know what they want. They're not gonna kill us before they get it."

They're not gonna kill *her*, anyway.

And I have to stay alive to make sure she gets out of this.

Just before opening my door, I reach down and drop something under the seat. We both climb out of her car and stand to face the dark-complected man with the gun. He's a wiry guy with prison tattoos and bad teeth. He points into the trees and snarls, "Walk. Dizz, move their car off the road."

Six looks at me and I give her a quick nod. She starts off down the slope. I start to follow her, but the wiry guy barks at me to stop. "Hands out to your sides."

Behind me, another guy moves up and starts to frisk me. It's only a matter of seconds before he finds my gun. Wiry guy flashes me a crooked grin. "Thought you were gonna get away with that, didn't ya?"

"Let's get on with this," I retort. "You want me to follow her, or not?"

"Go."

As we go, I note they're not bothering to hide their faces, or what they call each other. Either it hasn't occurred to them, or they aren't planning on letting us go afterwards.

I'm betting it's the latter.

We go about five-hundred yards until the wiry guy calls for us to stop. As we turn around, I notice a couple other people have joined us. One is a pale, angular ginger whose face is a war zone of freckles. The other is a woman, with bleach-fried blond hair and too much makeup on.

"What do you want with us?" Six demands in a loud, clear voice. "Why don't you just tell us?"

"You know what we want, honey," the woman sneers. "And don't think we won't do whatever it takes to get it."

"Lexxi," the ginger guy grunts. "Shut up."

"We don't even know who you are," Six insists. "How would we know what you want?"

"Flash wasn't enough of a message for you, Stacia?" wiry guy snaps, pointing the gun at my head. "You need another reminder?"

Six makes a low, fearful sound in her throat.

"Flash," she mutters dully. "So you're the ones who killed him."

"Flash betrayed us," the ginger says. "He knew what he was getting into. He knew as soon as we got out of the pen, he was finished. That's why he ran." He grimaces, showing a row of small, gray teeth. "And led us straight to you."

"What do you want with me?" Six cries. "I don't understand."

"The key," Lexxi drawls. "Flash didn't have it on him. And we know you're his girlfriend."

"Ex-girlfriend," Six corrects. "And I haven't seen him in years! He just showed up. He's been stalking me. I didn't know why!"

"You better hope you're lying," Ginger drawls. "Cause us getting that key back is the only thing keeping you alive."

"What's so special about this key, anyway?" I ask, cocking my head. "Whatever it is that's locked up, why don't you just force the lock? Blow it open?"

"It's to a safe deposit box," Lexxi spits back. "Can't exactly bust it open in a bank, now can we?"

"Lexxi, shut up!" wiry guy growls. "Jesus!"

"That seems like a bad place to store something valuable if you need to get to it quickly," I observe.

Ginger snorts and rolls his eyes. "Yeah," he mutters. "No shit. Letting Flash take care of hiding the jewels was a big fucking mistake. Leave it to his dumb ass to choose a goddamn *bank*." The wiry guy looks pissed. I get the feeling this is a bone of contention between them.

"I don't have the key," Six insists. She raises her hands in a supplicating gesture. "And I don't know where it is."

"Why the fuck should we believe you?" the wiry guy retorts. "Grimm. Lexxi. Search them. If it ain't on them, we'll just have to *convince* them to tell us where it is."

Six makes a strangled noise. I know she's on the verge of losing control. I have to do whatever it takes to keep her calm.

"It's okay, babe," I murmur. "Deep breaths."

The ginger, whose name is apparently Grimm, steps forward. I resist the urge to clock him in the jaw. Lexxi moves to Six. She tells Six to remove her shoes, and then her jacket. Six shoots me a worried look.

"What the fuck is this?" Lexxi asks with a frown as she examines the jacket. She feels the lining where Six has sewn it back together with dental floss. As she does, her mouth opens in shock and then elation. "Holy fuck!" she yells, her voice echoing through the trees. "It's here! It's right here! I got the key!"

Just then, a shot rings out, and then a volley. I barely have time to register what the sound is when Grimm is on the ground. I launch myself at Six and tackle her, bringing us both down and out of the range of fire behind a tree. I yell at her to stay down and crawl on my elbows over to the motionless Grimm. I find a gun tucked into a waist holster and pull it off him. Just then, the second guy and the chick bolt away and make a run for it. Taking aim at the guy, I fire at his calf and bring him down on one leg. A second shot hits him in the back, and he falls forward into the dead leaves. Off in the distance, a few more shots. Then a familiar voice rings out.

"Bullet!" Angel calls.

"Here!"

I run over to where Six is lying as half a dozen of my brothers emerge through the trees. She's unhurt, but shaking and bewildered. As I help her to her feet, she falls against me, trembling like a leaf.

"It's over, babe," I murmur against her hair.

"H—how did they find us?"

"GPS. I left my phone in the car."

Angel approaches us, flanked by Thorn and Beast. "Brother. You okay?" He glances over at Six.

I nod. "Yeah. Thanks to you. It was lookin' a little hairy for a bit." I look down at Six, who is still clinging to me like a lifeline. This is —"

"Stacia," she inserts, swallowing. "Thank you for saving us."

"All in a day's work, little lady," Thorn chimes in with a roguish look.

"Who the fuck are you, Robin Hood?" I grouse at him, trying not to smirk.

"What were these dickheads after, anyway?" Beast asks, looking around at the bodies lying on the forest floor.

"Oh! My jacket!" I feel Six's body stiffen as she glances around in alarm. "Lexxi has it!"

As if on cue, Gunner emerges from the trees with her. Lexxi is wearing the jacket, and trying without success to wrench her arm away from him.

"Caught this one trying to get away."

Lexxi gives him a venomous look and continues to struggle against his grip.

"Look, you," I snarl, stepping up to her. "You oughta be thanking your lucky stars you ain't dead."

"Fuck you," she hisses. I just laugh.

"I'll take that jacket now," Six says beside me.

Gunner lets go of her arm just long enough to pull it off of her and hand it to us. "What the fuck is so special about a jacket?" he frowns.

"Long story. I'll tell you later."

Six turns it inside out to look at the lining. "The key's still here," she says, holding it out so I can see it's still sewn shut. "She must not have had time to pull it out."

"Good," I nod. "We're good to go here, then."

Angel looks around in disgust at the bodies littering the ground. "We're gonna have to do some cleanup here."

Still glaring at Gunner, Lexxi seems to realize the gravity of her situation. "What are you gonna do to me?" she asks.

"You're a witness, bitch," Beast growls. "What do you *think* we're gonna do to you?"

Lexxi's face pales. "You can't! Please don't kill me!" She starts to cry, her voice rising to a wail. "Please!"

"Shut up," I cut her off. We ain't gonna kill her, but she doesn't need to know that yet. "Give me one good reason why we should give a shit what you want?"

Six puts a hand on my arm. "I have an idea."

I look at her and she continues.

"I'm pretty sure Lexxi here might be able to buy a ride for herself back to civilization with us," she says. "For the price of what she knows about this key. And her silence."

SIX

In the days after the shoot-out, I tried to forget about the bank box of jewels that had ended up costing so many people their lives. But try as I might, I couldn't put it out of my mind completely.

Part of it might have been that the key to the box was still stitched into the lining of my leather jacket. And the jacket, of course, was my one remaining physical reminder of Flash. He had been a terrible boyfriend, and an even worse ex-boyfriend. But he had been alive once, and I found myself remembering some of the good times we'd had, few as they were. Things I'd long since forgotten. He was a man who had grown up poor, and made a lot of terrible decisions in his life. In some ways, he wasn't that different from me or Bullet in that respect. In a strange kind of way, I found myself mourning his passing.

Once it was all over, I realized I no longer had to go by the nickname Six. When Bullet introduced me to Angel, the president of his club, I decided I wanted my life back. And that included my name. I felt like I'd earned it. So, for the first time in years, I introduced myself as Stacia.

Six, it turned out, was the *final* number of times I would go on the run.

WITH THE PERMISSION OF ANGEL, Bullet introduced me to Tweak, the Lords' resident hacker. Tweak and I spent a good part of the next few weeks holed up in his cave-like computer room at the clubhouse, brainstorming ways to track down the location and owner of the safe deposit box. All Lexxi had been able to tell us before the Lords finally let her go was that Flash was the one who set up the account, and only he and the other two men had known which bank it was.

Part of me wanted to let it go, and let the box sink into oblivion at the dusty back of a bank vault. But another part of me needed to see what was in it that had caused so much trouble. Besides, I didn't have a whole lot else to do during my non-work hours, anyway.

The rest of the Lords got used to my presence in their space pretty quickly. Apart from some good-natured flirting, they mostly left me be. I wasn't sure how much Bullet's influence had to do with that, but I was grateful for it.

It took us a while, but we eventually figured out which bank Flash had the safe deposit box with. Tweak and I started by looking at the records of all the banks within a five-mile radius of the apartment he was living in at the time. Thankfully, it didn't take long to find his name as an account holder, at a local branch of one of the large banks in the city.

When I see his name and the correct address come up on the monitor, I let out a whoop of excitement that makes Tweak chuckle and hold up his hand for a high five.

"Okay, then," he grins. "So, we probably have the bank. What do we do next?"

I hadn't thought that far yet. But as soon as the words are out of his mouth, an idea comes to me.

"I think I've got a plan," I say, smiling at the screen.

MY IDEA REVOLVES around the fact that Flash's real, full name is Sam Randall. Not *Samuel* Randall, mind you. Just Sam. That's the name his account is under at the Third National Bank.

Which makes it just a tiny bit easier for Tweak and me to forge identity documents and adopt his social security number as *Samantha* Randall.

Tweak and Bullet accompany me up to the city, armed with the key to the box. I have a new fake drivers license in my bag, complete with a name and address that matches the one on the bank account. I'm nervous as hell on the ride up, but I do what I can not to show it. I must run over all the things that could possibly go wrong in this scenario a thousand times during the drive. But amazingly, it ends up being almost ridiculously easy to get access to the safe deposit box. The teller barely even looks at my license when I tell her what I'm there for. She just gives me a brief, professional smile, and calls another employee to take me back to the deposit box area.

Tweak decided to wait out in the car, but Bullet comes with me for emotional support. He left his Lords of Carnage cut in the trunk, and even wore a long-sleeve flannel shirt that conceals the majority of his tattoos. As a result, he looks as nondescript as it's possible for a six-four, ruggedly handsome biker to be.

The bank employee who comes out to greet us leads us down a sterile, dark hallway to a reinforced steel door that must lead to the safe deposit boxes. We wait as he unlocks it and motions for us to go in ahead of him. The room we find ourselves in is lined floor to ceiling with more than a hundred numbered drawers. There's nothing else in the vault except a large table in the center. It's easily ten degrees colder in here than it is out in the main room of the bank, and I can't help but shiver.

Bullet and I watch as the bank employee goes to one of the numbered boxes, and inserts his key in one of the two keyholes in the door. I produce mine and turn it in the second lock, then pull gently. The door swings open.

"I'll be outside," he tells us. "Let me know when you've finished." Then, giving us a quick, wordless nod, he exits the room to give us our privacy.

I grasp the handle of the box inside and pull it out. It's heavy, but not much heavier than I would expect it to be if it was empty.

"Oh, my God," I breathe. "I can't believe this is happening."

"You can always lock it back up and walk away, you know. Whatever's in there, you're not under any obligation to do anything about it." Bullet says.

"No. I want to see what's in it." I reach out and splay my fingers across the top of the cold metal. "I want to see what's cost so much trouble, and so many lives."

I lift the lid, noticing my hand is trembling slightly. Inside is a large manila envelope with a metal closure. I pull it out, then pry up the wings of the clasp. Holding it over the table, I gently shake the contents onto the surface.

What falls out are an assortment of loose gems. None of them are in rings or any other setting. There are about a dozen of them: some diamonds, what look to be topaz, and a few emeralds.

"Huh," Bullet mutters. "This ain't that much. Maybe ten-thousand dollars' worth. Fifteen."

"Really?" I have no idea what jewels are worth, having never owned anything but costume jewelry. I frown. "That seems odd. Ten thousand doesn't seem like nearly enough for Flash to be trying to keep Grimm and Paco's share for himself."

"Unless there used to be more. Maybe Flash had been selling the gems while Grimm and Paco were in the pen." Bullet snorts softly. "That'd explain why he was coming after you by himself, instead of doing it with their help. That dumb shit probably knew they'd kill his ass if they found out part of it was gone. Maybe he wanted to grab what was left of the gems and leave the state. Or the country."

I contemplate his words. "He did seem pretty scared at the prospect of meeting up with them again. I couldn't figure out why at the time. It didn't make sense. But now it sort of does."

I pick up one of the larger diamonds and hold it up to the light. It's beautiful — shimmering, hard, nearly indestructible. I've never held a real diamond before. This thing would make one hell of an engagement ring for a rich socialite. "I wonder where these came from."

"Not likely we'd be able to figure that out, unless they're registered," Bullet tells me. "If the diamonds are certified, there'll be a serial number inscribed on then with a laser. If not, they're not really traceable. That's why they were removed from their settings."

"How would we find out if they're inscribed?"

"Tweak ought to know someone who can check that out for us."

Bullet watches impassively as I scoop the gems back into the envelope and seal it back up. I slide it into the inner pocket of my jacket and close the empty safe deposit box, turning my key to lock it.

"What are you gonna do with the gems?" he asks me.

"I have no idea," I admit. "I sure don't want to keep them. It feels wrong to sell them. But if what you say is true, we might never be able to find the owners they were stolen from. Besides which, I don't exactly want them calling the cops on me if they don't believe I'm not the one who stole them in the first place."

"Let's just take first things first," Bullet suggests. "First, we find out if they're registered, and then we go from there. But the choice is yours. You were the one who was in danger because of them. You're the one who had to uproot your entire life and leave everything behind over and over to keep yourself safe. You choose what to do with them next."

When we get back to the clubhouse to drop off the car, Tweak waves goodbye and heads inside. Bullet takes my hand and leads me to his Harley. I get on the back. But instead of taking me back to my apartment, he heads in the direction of his place.

I don't argue. I'm not in the mood to be alone right now, and I'm still processing what it means that I have several thousand dollars in gems in my jacket pocket.

Almost as soon as we're in the door, I'm in Bullet's arms and he's carrying me to bed. All the tension and fear of the last few hours melt away as he makes love to me, long and slow.

"You're so fucking wet," he rasps as he lowers himself onto the bed beside me, settling between my legs.

The heat of him is slick, delicious torture as he brushes his erection against me. My hips buck, straining toward him. A low, desperate moan wrenches from my throat. He teases me, bringing me to the edge with slow, deliberate strokes against my clit. Leaning forward to tower over me, his mouth finds one breast, and his tongue begins to flick and caress the nipple in the same rhythm. It drives me wild, and I wrap my legs around his waist, angling myself, rocking against his cock head as the pulse between my legs gets deeper and more insistent.

"You drive me fucking crazy, Stacia," he mutters against my skin, which turns electric at his touch and at the sound of my name, my *real* name, on his lips. My body is on fire for him, every word setting me further ablaze. "I need you. I fucking need you, now," he growls. He rears back, just long enough for me to open my eyes and take in the splendid, muscular beauty of him. He takes his cock in his fist and I whimper at the sight, my mouth watering with the urge to take him like that, to taste him, to make him lose control. But I know that will have to come later. With his other hand, he grasps my hip and pulls me to him. Then, with a flex of his thighs, he sheathes himself inside me.

I shudder, loving the fullness, how he stretches me to my limit. How every movement, no matter how small, sends tingles pulsing through me. His first thrusts are slow, but soon they're speeding up, becoming harder, more demanding. Deep inside me, his cock hits a spot that makes me come unraveled, crazy with need. I won't last long like this, can't last long, and I can only pant and gasp and hold on for dear life as I get ready to shatter into a million pieces around him.

"Fuck, baby, fuck, I'm close, you've got me so close... Jesus, yes, come with me," he urges, and his voice is like a flame licking me everywhere at once, making me obey his every word. I open my mouth to answer him, *yes*, but suddenly the dam breaks and I'm crying out as the waves crash over me and Bullet explodes inside me, filling me with everything he's got as he roars his release.

Afterwards, I lie in his arms, working to catch my breath and clinging to him as though he's the only thing tethering me to this earth. For at least the hundredth time, I marvel at how there's never been anyone like him for me. All other men pale in comparison, both in and out of the bedroom. Ever since our first night together, I've tried to tell myself it's just good sex, but I know that's not true. I've never wanted anyone the way I want him. I've just always assumed I couldn't possibly have him. Not like that, anyway. And now...

In spite of myself, my throat tightens, and for a second I'm afraid I'm going to cry. I must make a noise, because Bullet hears it and pulls me closer. "What's up, babe?"

I swallow a couple of times, until I'm sure I can trust my voice. "I'm just thinking about everything that's happened," I murmur, lifting one shoulder in a shrug. *It's sort of true*, I tell myself. *I'm just leaving out some of it.* "It's just weird to realize I don't have to run anymore. I've never really thought about how it would feel to be able to settle down. Maybe even put down roots here."

"Glad to hear you're thinking of sticking around," he rumbles.

I can't quite read his tone, and that makes me cowardly.

"I mean, at least for a while, anyway," I add, trying to sound casual. "Chance has said I'm ready to start working unsupervised as a tattoo artist, and he's hoping to move me up to full-time in a few months if business stays good. If he still wants me, that is," I can't help but add, my mood turning dark.

"Why wouldn't he?"

"Well, I mean... I'm gonna have to tell Chance, Dez, and everyone else my real name, and what my story is." Somehow, even though the danger was over weeks ago, I haven't been able to bring myself to do this yet. The thought of what their reactions might be has stopped me every time. "I'll have to tell them I've been lying to them all this time," I continue, feeling sick. "Maybe they won't trust me once they know. After all, they're going to find out I've been a stranger all along. What if they don't want to know the real me?"

"They already know you, babe," he says softly. "A name's

just a name. They'll adjust. Besides, didn't you say Hannah already knows your story?"

"Only the bare bones," I protest. "Besides, even I didn't know the real reason Flash was stalking me when I told her. I just told her I had a crazy ex-boyfriend."

"Have faith in them. They're not gonna think any different of you."

I sigh and snuggle against him, still doubtful but wanting to believe him. "Maybe you're right," I murmur softly.

Maybe nothing has to change. Maybe Bullet's right, and I can just go on living my life here in Tanner Springs as Stacia Edison, formerly known as Six. A month ago, that would have been an unimaginable dream come true. A fantasy that I could barely ever hope to attain. But now...

A normal life. The chance to put down roots. To have real friends. Friends I don't have to keep any secrets from.

It's almost too perfect. Just about everything I want out of life, handed to me on a silver platter. Except for one thing.

Now that it's all over, I don't know where Bullet and I stand. He's helped me get my life back, and I've never been more grateful to anyone than I am to him.

But as he takes me in his arms again, I realize it's more than that. It's more than gratitude I feel for him. More than sexual attraction, too, although there's certainly that.

The fact is... I'm pretty sure I've fallen in love with him.

Bullet is an enigma. Charming and cocky, brooding and closed off. He's kind when I expect him to be hard, rough and demanding in a way I've never known before and have come to crave. His eyes bore into my soul when he takes my body. The touch of his tongue on my lips is electric. The rough slide of his thumb against my clit sends me into spasms of pure pleasure. I've come to trust him more than I've ever trusted any man — hell, more than any *person* — I've ever known.

And yet, I have no idea how he feels about me. Not really.

When I was still worrying about how long I'd have before I'd be forced to leave Tanner Springs, the question of how I felt about him was one I refused to let enter my mind.

But now? I can't push it away anymore. I'm lost to him. I'm lost to this.

That night — exhausted by everything that's happened that day — I sleep the sleep of the dead. As I drift off, feeling safe and warm in Bullet's arms, I allow myself to believe in a future for us. Just for tonight. Even as I tell myself that whatever has already happened between us is enough.

It will *have* to be enough, if he doesn't feel the same way.

THE NEXT MORNING, I wake up, and it seems like everything has already changed.

Bullet isn't lying beside me. Instead, he's already dressed and standing in the bedroom doorway, his leather cut covering the muscled shoulders that only last night I gripped as I came in his arms.

"You're awake," I mumble, heaving myself into a sitting position as I draw the covers up around my breasts. I push a messy lock of hair out of my eyes and take him in. "Is something wrong?"

In two strides, he's crossed the room and sits down on the edge of the bed beside me. There's a grim look on his face that I've never seen before. Not even when he was dealing with Flash and the others.

"Six. Stacia. Dammit, I don't know what to call you anymore." His frustration is an impatient storm on his face.

"What is it? What's wrong?" I glance down, and notice his phone is in his hand.

"Nothing's wrong, exactly. I just have something to ask you." He rubs a hand roughly over his face. If he slept last night, it doesn't show, because he looks exhausted. "A favor, I guess. And I hate like hell to do it."

My heart sinks slowly down to my stomach. Though I tell myself I have no right to be upset.

Bullet helped me.

Now he's asking for me to pay him back.

Tit for tat. Quid pro quo. That's all it is.

I don't even hesitate. Because I *do* owe him. I owe him my life, in more ways than one.

But also because I'd do anything for him. Anything to be near him.

"Of course," I say around the lump forming in my throat. "Anything you need."

SIX

"You won't be in any danger," Bullet assures me. "I'll make sure of that."

All the way to the clubhouse on the back of his bike, Bullet had kept silent about what he was about to ask me to do. He told me he wanted to explain the whole thing here, with the other Lords around. He said it would help me understand what the plan was, and what my role would be if I accepted it. Bullet assured me that once I'd heard everything and asked all the questions I wanted to, I could refuse if I wanted to, and he wouldn't ask me twice.

But one look at the creases of exhaustion on his forehead —

the rough, angry way he runs his hand through his close-cropped hair — and I know I'll say yes. No matter what he's about to ask me. Because I might not know Bullet all that well, and I don't know exactly where we stand. But I do know that he wouldn't ask a hard thing of me unless he really needed it.

"So... you want me to pretend to be... what? A prostitute?" My mouth stumbles over the word as I look around the room. I scan the faces of the Lords present — men I'm only just barely coming to know. There's Tank and Striker, who I first met at the Smiling Skull. There's also Lug Nut, Gunner, and Hawk. All of them, Bullet has told me, are working with him to bring down the man he calls Ellis Strickland.

"Not a prostitute," Bullet corrects me. "A decoy."

"To help you find your stepfather."

"We've found him already," Tank chimes in. "More or less, anyway. We've got a guy who's made contact for us. We just need to get at him in person. This is the best way we've figured out to do that."

"Why is it so hard to meet with him?" I search Bullet's features.

"Ellis — he goes by Edge, now — is cagey. He's careful about who he meets with, for good reason. The shit he gets up to is dangerous. He's made a lot of enemies." Bullet shows his teeth in a rictus of a smile that makes my blood run cold. "And he's under the protection of a powerful criminal organization that we can't go head to head with. You don't need to know who that is. So we need to figure out a different way to smoke him out into the open. Something that will get him to let his guard down."

"Me," I supply quietly.

"Not you in person. Pictures of you." Bullet pauses, a flick of what looks like regret crossing his face. "But yeah. One of Edge's current businesses is supplying rich, depraved fuckers with pretty young women they can take their pleasure with.

These clients of his have some very... *particular* tastes. So, going through the usual channels is risky for them."

"What do you mean, particular tastes?"

Bullet's jaw works as he mulls his words. It's clear he's struggling to think of a way to put this.

"Let's just say... the girls they supply tend to be young, with no family or connections. Kids who aren't likely to be missed."

Oh my God. "Are you saying... what I think you're saying?" I choke.

Bullet's eyes lock on mine. His pupils are dark as coal. "Yeah, I am. His clients get off on torture. Rape. Using the girls like objects, to do with them what they please. Then discarding them if necessary."

"And as you can imagine," Lug Nut growls in a deep voice, "the human garbage that likes that shit will pay huge money for it. This Edge guy has found himself quite a fuckin' cash cow."

"And you want me to pose for photos to lure him in?" I'm suddenly freezing, as though the temperature has dropped fifty degrees in this room. I hug my arms to my chest to ward off the chill, but it's no use. The cold is coming from inside me.

"Nothing too racy. Just enough to convince them you exist, and you're up for sale." Bullet reaches out, cupping his hand gently under my chin. "You're never in any danger, Six. You won't get anywhere near them. We just need to convince them that we have a product worth selling."

And I'm the product.

A tremor goes through me as I contemplate his words. I knew, abstractly, that such dark corners of the world exist. But as much as my life has brushed against certain criminal elements, I've never been exposed to anything as horrible as this. It's almost impossible for me to wrap my head around the fact that a man like this was once Bullet's stepfather. The thought of such a man looking at photographs of me — licking his lips, imagining how much money he could make from selling me off to one of his monstrous clients — sends my stomach churning. For a few seconds, I think I might vomit. I suck in a breath, then another, trying to calm my suddenly racing pulse.

But then I remember that there are actual girls out there who are being sold to these predators by him. Those girls are actually being beaten, tortured, raped. Killed, even.

I'm just being asked to provide a few pictures as bait. To help them catch him.

"What will you do with him when you get him?" I whisper.

"Stop him." His voice is cold as steel. "Finish him."

Blinking, I gaze up into his eyes. The expression I see there is so flat, so dead, it tells me more than words ever could. They're the eyes of a man who feels no remorse. Who will stop at nothing until his own justice, his own vengeance, has been served.

The other men are silent. All of them look at me, expectantly.

I know Bullet won't ask me twice if I say no.

But I also know that's not an option for me.

"When do we start?" I ask.

THEY BRING in a woman to take the pictures. Her name is Samantha, and Bullet introduces her to me as Hawk's old lady. She's a professional photographer in town. She's stunningly beautiful, with glossy black hair and dark eyes. She also looks to be about four or five months pregnant.

"Thought it'd be easier for you if it was a woman," Bullet says gently. "And she'll know what to do. How to make the photos look authentic. Convincing."

"Call me Sam," Samantha smiles. She produces a plastic bag and hands it to me. "I brought some clothes for you to change into. We'll go into one of the back rooms to do the shoot. It'll be just you and me, so don't be nervous. It'll go quickly, I promise."

I take the bag and peer into it. "I didn't think we'd need to do professional photos for this. Isn't that going a little overboard?"

"The point isn't to make them look professional," she answers, giving me a wink. "It's to make them look *un*professional. Authentic, in a way that won't arouse any suspicions. But still tempting enough to reel them in. That can be harder than you'd think."

"Huh. Okay."

"Come on." Sam leads me toward the back of the clubhouse, into a room that looks like it's largely used for storage. "I'm having Hawk and Lug Nut bring in some lighting equipment for me." She pats her slightly swollen belly. "I'm totally capable of doing it myself, but Hawk won't hear of me lifting anything heavy," she sighs, but there's a twinkle in her eye.

"How far along are you?"

"Twenty weeks. You'd think I was at term, the way Hawk hovers around me. He's pretty much made me promise to do any shoots that need artificial lighting in my home studio." She chuckles. "It's fair enough, I guess. It is our first biological child."

"Biological?" I ask, liking Sam already.

"We have a ten-year-old boy. Adopted." She giggles. "Though you'd never know it, the way he takes after Hawk. In mannerisms, especially. That boy is his mini-me, through and through." As she talks, Sam is looking around, evaluating the space we're in. She cocks her head and points toward the far wall, which is made of brick but painted a dark, tar black. "I'm going to have the men bring one of the old sofas from the game room in here, to put against that wall. You can go change in that room," she says, pointing toward a half-open door. "Come out when you're ready. I'll want to put some make-up on you, mess with your hair a little before we start shooting. Take your time."

I do as she says, going into a small room that turns out to be a storage closet. I feel along the wall for a light switch and turn it on. There's not much in here but boxes about the size of paper ream boxes. I close the door, set the plastic bag down on one of them, and pull out the clothes. They're raggedy, cheap-looking, and skimpy — a black tank top, plaid schoolgirl skirt, fishnets. At the bottom of the bag is a pair of black Doc Marten-style boots. I strip off my own clothes and pull everything on, slowly. When I get to the tank top, I start to pull it over my bra, but then think better of it and take the bra off. Though I feel more exposed, I think back to what Sam said about this needing to look authentic. If I'm to help Bullet, that's what I need to do.

When I open the door of the closet and walk back out into the room, the men are helping Sam set up her lighting. The couch is there now, shoved up against the wall. Lug Nut is bent over, screwing a tall, black umbrella thing into a metal stand on the floor. He straightens, and when his eyes fall on me a shadow passes over them.

"Son of a bitch," he spits out in a choked voice. Then, as I gape at him, he turns on his heel and stomps out of the room without another word.

Sam, who's been fiddling with a camera hanging around her neck, looks up and watches him leave, then pivots toward me. "Oh. Shit," she murmurs quietly.

"What's wrong with Lug Nut?" I ask her, bewildered. "Did I do something wrong?"

"No, no. It's nothing like that," Sam explains apologetically. "I think maybe this whole situation has got him on edge a little bit. It's not your fault."

"Why is he upset?"

"Bad memories. Lug Nut's old lady, Eden, was once pimped

out by an ex-boyfriend. They got her hooked on heroin and held her in a shitty old motel room. That's how Lug Nut met her, in fact. He and Gunner managed to get her out before..." Sam trails off. "Well. *Before*."

"Oh my God."

"Yeah. She's okay now, though." Sam gives me a reassuring smile. "Gunner's mom got her off the dope. But I think this whole thing is bringing back some shit for Lug Nut, you know?"

"God, I can only imagine." How horrible.

"Gunner's wife Alix is Eden's sister, by the way. You'll meet them. They're both really nice." Sam pulls the camera off over her head and sets it on a low stool beside her. "Okay, come over here. Let me put some makeup on you."

Sam brings me over to the couch, adjusts the lighting, and then opens up a small case with a bunch of makeup palettes inside. She brings out some heavy concealing makeup, and tells me she's going to start by covering up my visible tattoos.

"We want to make you look as young as possible," she explains as she dabs at my arm. I watch in fascination as the intricate tattoo on my forearm begins to disappear. "This will take a bit, but when I'm done, it'll be a lot easier to do the touch-ups on the photos themselves."

I sit in silence as she works, contemplating what she told me about Alix and Eden. It's sweet that Sam just assumes I'll meet them at some point. She must think Bullet and I are together — like *together* together. Permanently. I think about telling her my doubts, but realize it feels too painful to bring up. Listening to her tell me what my heart is dying to hear would just make things worse. Better to just concentrate on what I'm doing right now. Right now, my job is to help him, no matter what the outcome is for us.

Once Sam is satisfied with my makeup, she has me go through a series of poses on the couch — some lying down, some scrunched up into one corner, some with me looking away from the camera. Sam tells me that what she's going for is not an overtly sexy look.

"You're young, and afraid. You don't want to do this. You're being forced to." She pauses, and purses her lips. "Remember that the men we're trying to sell you to get off on fear. On domination."

"God. This is just... awful."

"I know," she says grimly. "That's why it's important."

The shoot itself takes a little over half an hour. Sam shows me the photos afterwards, flipping through them on her camera as I peer at the screen. As horrifying as they are, I have to admit she's done a fantastic job. She's managed to make me look sexy and afraid at the same time. The low, oblique light she's used in some of the closer-up shots make my pupils look huge, like maybe I'm on drugs. All in all, they're extremely convincing.

"They used to call this look 'heroin chic,'" Sam tells me in a dry tone. "In the nineties, looking too thin and drugged out was considered the gold standard for fashion models. How's that for gross?"

"I feel like I need a shower," I admit. This whole thing has taken a lot more out of me than I thought it would.

"I know." Sam looks at me, biting her lip, and then reaches over and gives me a warm hug. "You did great, though," she murmurs. "And don't worry. We'll print a few of these for the men to use, and all the files will be destroyed. Once this is all over, there will be no evidence this shoot ever happened, I promise."

"Thank you," I say, grateful.

Sam sends me out to change back into my clothes. A few minutes later, I re-emerge just in time to see Hawk come in, with Bullet trailing behind him. "All done?" Hawk asks, slipping his arm around her.

"Yep. Check these out." Sam holds up the camera so Hawk

can look at the display. She thumbs through a few of them, and he lets out a whistle, impressed.

"Check these, out, Bull," he says. Bullet leans in and takes a look. I watch him, hoping he'll be impressed, too. But as he looks through one image after another, his face darkens.

"Yeah. That'll do." His eyes flick to me, expressionless. "Thanks," he says gruffly.

"No problem," I say meekly.

As soon as the words are out of my mouth, he turns to Sam. "I gotta take care of a couple things here. Could you drive her home for me?"

"Sure, no problem," she replies.

Bullet turns and half-storms out of the room, almost like Lug Nut did earlier. I want to follow him to ask him if anything's wrong, but I don't have the guts. It's like my feet are glued to the floor.

Sam doesn't seem to notice anything. "Just let me get this equipment broken down," she says to me kindly. "Hawk, baby, can you help me load this stuff into the car?" She glances at the exercise tracker on her wrist. "Ooh, perfect timing! I have just enough time to get to school to pick up Connor after I drop you off."

When we emerge back into the main room of the clubhouse, Bullet is nowhere to be seen. With a last glance behind me, I follow Sam outside and get in her car. I give her directions to my apartment, and do my best to keep up my end of the conversation as she chatters away — all the while, trying not to wonder whether this is how Bullet and I end.

21

BULLET

S am goes home and spends some time messing with the photos she took of Six. A few hours later, Hawk comes back to the clubhouse with a large envelope in his hands. He spreads the prints of five photos out on the table in front of Tank, Striker, and me. These are the best ones, Hawk tells us.

"They're good," Tank remarks. He picks one up and examines it more closely. "Damn."

"'Course they are," Hawk rumbles. "Sam's the best at what she does. I knew she'd have an eye for this."

"Not just her. Stacia is a fuckin' actress. It's fuckin' freaky." Striker lets out a low whistle. "Jesus. These pictures are convincing as hell. If I didn't know better..."

They're right. The pictures *are* good. Almost too good. Sam has made Six look beautiful and arresting, of course, which she already is. Any idiot with a camera could capture that.

But there's something more to it. They're sexy as hell, but in a way that is somehow deeply fucking disturbing. Pretty white girls like Six are at a premium for this kind of shit. And considering what his clients get off on, they'll pay top fucking dollar for the right one. These photos are perfect in that respect. Six looks exactly the sort of girl a sick fuck like that would be attracted to. A would-be predator's fantasy prey. Sam has made her look helpless and vulnerable. Fragile. Haunted, even. The girl who stares out at me from these photos knows that no one is coming to save her from the fate that awaits her. She knows she's been abandoned — that she's no longer anything but an object, to be used, and abused, and thrown away.

It makes me sick to look at this picture and think of Six in that position. And I about want to rip my fuckin' hair out thinking about Ellis looking at these photos of her. My stomach roils at the idea of him planning to sell her as a fucking sex slave, to a man who would get off on terrorizing her.

A lot of these girls are only used a handful of times, I know. Some of them, just once. Each of them is worth a fortune. And at the same time, they're worthless. Completely deprived of their humanity. It adds a depth and dimension to my fury that threatens to overwhelm me.

Thick bile rises in my throat. As much as I hated Ellis after my mother burned to death, the rage and fury I feel now is a hundred times worse.

When I kill Ellis — and I *will* kill him — it will be for even looking at these pictures of Six and seeing her as an object and nothing more.

"Remember. It's me who ends him," I remind my brothers, my voice hard as a diamond cutting through glass. "No one else."

THAT NIGHT, I don't go to Six. I can't touch her right now. I'm too disgusted with myself. I can't fucking deal with the fact that I'm using her body to get at my stepfather. As I lie in my own bed, alone, I stare up at the ceiling, but all I can see is her face in those photographs. Even now, they're being served up to whet the appetites of some perverted fuck with money. I feel sick to my fuckin' stomach about the whole goddamn thing. Even though it's to help catch a man who doesn't deserve to live, and wipe him off the face of this earth. I hate that I've gotten her involved in my shit.

There had to have been another way to get to Ellis. A better way. But I chose this. And Six probably agreed because she felt like she didn't have any choice.

I used her. And now, because of that, my fucking stepfather will look at her like an object. He'll get hard looking at her, and thinking about all the fucking money she'll make him.

"*Fuck!*" I roar into the darkness.

How am I any better than he is?

THE NEXT DAY, I'm at the clubhouse in the game room late in the afternoon. I'm on pins and fucking needles waiting for word from the contact who brought Ellis the photos of Six.

Ellis/Edge is careful as hell, as anyone who deals in this kind of crime has to be. There can't be a digital footprint of any part of this transaction. It's not as easy as loading up the images onto a website like Backpage, or emailing them to him. We had to have our contact courier the photos to one of his people, whose job it is to get them to him. It's the only way we can provide proof that we've got a girl with the look Edge wants for his client.

The waiting is making me goddamn crazy, so I'm trying to work out some of the frustration with a first-person shooter game. I've got the volume turned up so fucking loud I don't hear Striker calling my name until he and Tank are standing between me and the large TV screen mounted on the wall in front of me.

"Turn that shit off!" Striker yells, raising his hands in exasperation. "Goddamn!"

I hit pause on the controller and toss it onto the leather couch beside me.

"What?" I demand.

"We got a problem, brother."

Fuck. I stand and rake a hand over my scalp. "What is it?"

"Just got a message from our contact," he answers. "Edge is saying the photos aren't good enough. He's gonna send one of his guys to the meet-up in his place, to make sure this is legit."

"What the fuck?" I shout in frustration.

"The contact says Edge told him photos can be doctored. He wants to check out the goods in person. Says he needs to know that the girl in the pictures really exists, and that she looks like she does in the photos. The way it's gonna work is, his guy will come to the meet-up, and if he determines she's the real deal, he'll call Edge to come in person to check her out."

"Shit. Are you saying we need to bring Six with us?" I stare at him.

"Sounds like it." Tank looks grim. "But look, we can make it work. We can keep her safe."

"No."

"It's the only way we'll get Edge to come out in the open, Bull," Tank warns me.

"No." I shake my head firmly. "I can't do that. I can't fucking bring her into this anymore than I already have."

"We're in too deep now, brother," Tank protests. "If we don't bring Stacia, the deal falls through. We'll never get close to Edge."

"There's got to be another way."

"There isn't," Striker cuts in. "Not unless we start all over from zero. Look, he isn't gonna hurt Stacia, Bull. She's not valuable to her unless she's in perfect condition. So we just bring her in, let him look at her, see she's real, and then take her away. Tell him we're keeping her under wraps until the transaction is completed."

"No. No. I can't..." My mouth won't form the rest of the sentence. *I can't treat her like a fucking sex slave. I can't do that to her.* "Someone else," I say stubbornly. "We have to find someone else."

"Who else are you gonna get to do this?" Tank insists. "No girl, no Edge. You get that, right?" He taps his forehead with a finger, like I'm dense. "And he's seen her picture now. Stacia's who he's expecting. If you bring someone else, his guy won't bring Edge to us. Come on, Bullet. We're at the finish line! What the fuck? We can't back out now!"

"I said fucking no!" I explode at them both. "I'm not gonna ask Six to do this! End of fuckin' story!"

"Ask me to do what?"

Surprise mixing with dread in my gut, I wheel around to see Six standing in the doorway.

"What are you doing here?" I growl.

"Tweak called me in about the diamond registration thing." Six cocks her head, narrowing her eyes at the three of us. "What do you need me to do?"

"Nothing!"

"Bullet's stepdad says he won't come to the meet-up unless you're there in person," Tank pipes up.

"Goddamnit, Tank!" I yell, turning to glare at him.

"I'll do it," she says simply.

"No!" I roar.

"Bullet, stop! I said I'll do it."

I stride toward her, until I'm less than a foot away and facing her. I have to make her understand.

"It's not safe, Six! I fucking refuse to bring you any further into this. I've pulled you in too far already."

"That's exactly why I'm going to do it." Her voice is firm.

"What?" I gape at her, dumbfounded. "That makes no fucking sense."

"Yes it does," she says patiently. "Look, Bullet. You've told me enough about this man for me to know what my involvement in this represents. I can't help but think of how many girls are in real danger because of him, and the clients he serves. Think of how many of those girls might be saved if we do this."

"That's not why —"

"I don't care." She fixes me with a strong, direct stare that tells me she's not about to back down. "I don't care why you started this. What I care about is what it means to finish it. When you get to Edge — before you..." Six trails off, momentarily averting her eyes. But when she looks back at me, resolve is etched on her beautiful features. "Before you do whatever you plan to do with him, I want you to get the name of the client that he wants to buy me for. And then I want you to find him, too. Make sure he never, ever does anything like this to a girl or a woman again. That's my price."

"You know that's not why I started this," I warn her.

"I know," she says softly. "But that doesn't matter to me. What matters is what you're going to do to end it. And I want to be part of that." Six pauses. "I know if I ask you to do it, you will. So I'm asking. And that's why I'm going to help you. Because it's the right thing to do." She puts a hand on my forearm. "I'm doing this. You saved me once, Bullet. I know you'll keep me safe this time, too."

"No," I repeat, but even I can hear that I'm losing steam.

"Yes. It's a done deal, Bullet. So stop arguing. We're in this together."

Six breaks my gaze and turns to Tank and Striker.

"Okay. So, tell me what I need to do."

22

BULLET

"You nervous?" I ask her.

"A little," Six admits. She's dressed up and ready to go, in an outfit that looks similar to the one she was wearing for the photo shoot with Sam. This time she's got on a long-sleeve black mesh shirt over a black cami, a short skirt, and bare legs with platform heels that accentuate their shapeliness. Her hair is pulled back from her face. She's not wearing any makeup except for the stuff that's covering up her tattoos and some blush-colored lipstick. The end result is that she looks about sixteen years old, which of course is the idea.

Six looks jittery. Her face is pale, which accentuates the beauty of her fine features. I'm guessing she didn't sleep that well last night, judging from the hint of shadows under her eyes. She looks gorgeous and vulnerable. Perfect bait for the sick fuck we're trying to lure in.

Angel and Beast aren't here at the clubhouse with us. They're not going on the run; they're too well known as the prez and VP of the Lords of Carnage, so they could be recognized. It's just Tank, Striker, me, Tweak, and Lug Nut. We're all out of uniform, exchanging our cuts for suit coats that conceal our weapons. Tank is the lead — the one "selling" Six — and we're his bodyguards.

We all have to play our parts, and we have to be spot on, or the deal will fall through.

And if that happens, we all might be in danger. Especially Six.

Tank's heavy footsteps sound on the floorboards, and we all turn to see him. He's got on an expensive-looking suit, and shoes that probably cost more than my monthly fuckin' mortgage.

"Jesus fuck, Tank," Striker snickers. "You look like a fuckin' high-roller pimp."

"Yeah, which is exactly the point, numb nuts," Tank shoots back. His eyes glide to Six, and he gives her a satisfied once-over. "Nice get-up, darlin'. You'll do."

Six snorts and grins back at him. "You clean up pretty good, Tank. You almost look respectable." She cocks a brow and sniffs. "Cologne, too? You go all out."

"Why thank you," he shoots back, doffing an imaginary hat. "If you ever get tired of this fucker," he continues, indicating me, "you know where I am."

Six blushes a bit and glances over at me. I can't help but avert my gaze. I still feel shitty for bringing her into this. She basically fucking insisted, but I could have put my foot down. I should have put my foot down. Goddamnit.

But the fact is, we need her. *I* need her here, in order to pull this off.

"You, look good, too," Six breathes. "But weird. I barely recognize you."

"Good," I grunt. "That's the point."

As well as wearing this monkey suit get-up, I've shaved my head, and also removed my short, dark beard. In its place is a blond, mountain man beard that conceals my features. It's pretty fucking realistic, if I do say so myself, even though the adhesive itches like a motherfucker.

"You should have worn a wig, too," Six giggles. "You'd look like Grizzly Adams in a suit."

"Har, har. You're in a pretty fucking' jovial mood," I grouse, without knowing why. Jealousy, maybe. It doesn't sit right with me that she's letting Tank flirt with her. "Thought you said you were nervous."

"Of course I'm nervous. But this is how I cope with nervous." She gives me a searching look. "You okay?"

Fuck. "Yeah. I'm fine," I spit out, and turn away. It almost feels like I'm looking for reasons to pick a fight with her. I think in a way I want her to be mad at me. Hell, if she was mad enough, maybe she'd change her mind about doing this. And I wouldn't have any good reason to stop her if she walked out right now. Part of me wishes she would. I don't deserve her help. I shouldn't take it. I should be protecting the woman I love.

The woman I love.

Goddamnit, that's what's got me all the fuck out of sorts, isn't it? I love her. I am all the fuck the way in love with this beautiful, brave, gorgeous woman.

But fuck, right now I don't feel like I deserve her. Not one goddamn bit.

"Okay," Tank calls out. "Everyone get over here. Let's go over the plan one more time before we head out."

The group of us gathers around him. Six wraps her arms around her body protectively, and after a second walks over and grabs that damn leather jacket, pulling it on over her skimpy outfit. I resist the urge to put my arm around her to give her some extra warmth.

"We're all going in the limo together," Tank explains one final time, referring to the black Lexus with fake plates we have parked outside. "Tweak's the driver. The rest of you fuckers are around me at all times as my guards. Bullet is gonna hang back. He can't talk, since Edge might recognize his voice."

Tank looks at each of us one by one before continuing. "We don't make any moves until Edge is actually in the room, guard down, ready to make the transaction," he says. "Stacia is the priority. We keep her safe, and we get her out of there immediately if shit looks like it's starting to go south. The plan is to pull her out of there as soon as Edge has looked her over, so she's out of the way before we make a move. If shit goes to hell, the signal to act is when I say the word 'deal.' You all know what to do in that case: Stacia, you hit the ground, go for cover. Striker, Lug Nut, Tweak, you're guns out. Depending on how many men they have, you shoot to kill or to wound." Tank glances toward me. "Bullet and I grab Edge. We clear?"

A rumble of assent moves though the group. Six bites her lip and nods.

"Okay. Let's move."

THE MEET-UP POINT is a place we suggested. It's a stroke of fuckin' luck Ellis agreed to it. Assuming everything goes according to plan, it's perfect for what I have in mind for him. The pole barn used to have a farm house not far from it, but the house was in such bad shape the owners razed it a while ago.

The barn itself sits at the end of a long gravel driveway, on a parcel of land that's been for sale for a good amount of time — a few years, at least. I'm guessing any farmer worth his shit must know the land isn't worth much, or it would have sold by now.

A large black Lexus limousine pulling off on that driveway would probably raise a few eyebrows out here — if there were any eyebrows around to raise. As it is, there's not a person or a car in sight as we drive the half-mile of the driveaway and park in back of the pole barn, out of sight of the main road. We're the first ones here, about half an hour early. Tank sends Lug Nut and Striker to scope out the area, to make sure Ellis hasn't sent any snipers out ahead of time. They come back about ten minutes later, satisfied we're alone.

In the meantime, Tweak smashes the lock on the small side door and kick it open with his foot. We all file inside, until we're standing in the center of the space. It's empty except for some old cords of rotting wood, a few saw horses, and an ancient-looking riding lawn mower. There's not much light in the place — only one naked bulb hanging from a six-foot cord in the center of the ceiling — and it takes a bit for our eyes to adjust. When mine do, I turn to look at Six. She hasn't said a word since we arrived. Her face is tense, her eyes unfocused. Almost like she's withdrawn into herself.

"You okay?" I murmur.

She gives me an imperceptible little nod. "I'm fine." Her voice is distant. "Just let me be, Bullet."

We wait, mostly in silence. The time of the meet-up comes. Ten more minutes go by. I start to feel restless.

Suddenly, Tweak pipes up from the doorway. "They're here."

We get into position. I'm on one side of Tank, Lug Nut and Striker on the other. Six stands in the middle, next to Tank. We hear the crunch of tires on gravel. Then the slam of car doors.

A group of four men enters the pole barn. Tweak moves to stand on my side, in front of me. I resist the urge to reach up and check my beard.

"Gentlemen," Tank announces in a jovial voice. "Glad you could make it."

The tall one in the middle seems to be the one in charge. He's thin but wiry-looking, and heavily bearded, dressed in a black turtleneck under a black suit. He doesn't bother with formalities. "That's the girl," he intones, flicking his gaze to her.

"It is," Tank agrees. "A prime piece, if I do say so myself."

"How old?"

"She told me she was sixteen when we met," Tank says smoothly. "Though I suspect she might be younger."

The bearded guy takes a step forward. "She is a natural blond, yes?" he asks, looking her over.

"Yup." Tank flashes him a leer. "Above, and below. And the prettiest little snatch you've ever seen. Though I haven't sampled the goods. She's a virgin, tight little pussy, all ready for your boss."

I hear a tiny, strangled noise escape from Six's throat. I'm not sure whether she's acting or not. It sends a knife of regret through my gut. But either way, it fucking works. I watch, adrenaline beginning to flow through my veins, as Edge's man stares at her for a couple of seconds more, then blinks, seemingly satisfied. He reaches into his breast pocket and pulls out a phone. Taking a few steps back, he snaps a quick photo of Six, and presumably sends it to Ellis.

A moment later, he presses a button and holds the phone to his ear.

"Yeah. She's here. It's legit."

He listens for a second, grunts, and ends the call.

"Edge is coming."

He steps back and rejoins the men he came in with,

standing at almost military attention. He doesn't speak anymore, or even bother to look at us.

The silence in the barn has a weird, echoing character to it. My muscles are taut as the strings on a fucking violin. The adrenaline rushing through my veins feels like a drug, wiring me with tense anticipation.

Then, with a scrape, the door opens, and Ellis steps inside.

Fuck me. My former stepfather has come up in the world, that's for damn sure. As he strides toward us, I notice he's wearing a suit that's even more expensive than the one Tank has on. He's not wearing a tie, but the collar of his shirt looks starched enough to give someone a fuckin' paper cut. A signet ring adorns his left pinky. Even his haircut looks like it cost a mint. The fuckin' white trash asshole I knew back in the day is almost unrecognizable.

Almost. But it's him. It's fuckin' him, for sure.

And this is how he got his money. Buying and selling not only drugs, but people. My mother was just the first in a long line of people he has sacrificed to get where he is right now.

But that fucking ends. Right here. Right now.

If I was worried that Ellis would recognize me, there was no need. He barely looks at any of us except Tank. I realize it was a good call dressing him up the way we did. Ellis lusts after money. He respects people who have it. And now that he's one of them, Tank is the only person in this room who matters to him.

Well, Tank, and the girl he thinks he's about to purchase.

"I'm Edge," he says to Tank. The corners of his mouth spread into a humorless grin. His teeth are capped, gleaming white and overly straight in a way that makes him look even more like a predator.

"Murphy," Tank lies. He gestures toward Six. "Here she is. Exactly as ordered."

"Lovely. Perfect." When Ellis's eyes fall on Six, they practically flash dollar signs. He moves closer to her, fingers a stray lock of her hair that frames her pale face. "Where did you find her?"

"She was a runaway from foster care," Tank smirks. "Her parents are dead. I picked her up on the streets." He gives Six a lecherous leer. Tank moves next to the other man, and reaches a hand up to clasp Six's chin roughly. He angles her face up to his. "She was *desperate* for someone to protect her from the cold, cruel world. Isn't that right, sweetheart?" he croons.

Six flinches, and tries to pull her head away. But Tank holds her fast so she can't do it. Jesus, they're playing this so perfectly, I'm half convinced myself. The knife in my gut twists harder.

"She looks terrified, poor thing," Ellis murmurs, but he's grinning, lust fairly seeping from his pores.

"She's a virgin," Tank repeats, releasing Six's face. She sucks in a shuddering breath and looks away. "So innocent, so inexperienced. Well worth the price."

Ellis sneers. "I doubt my client will care one way or another." He moves closer to Six. She takes a tiny step back, but doesn't dare move any further. His face is inches from hers — so close I imagine she can smell his breath. "I'm afraid your new master isn't very nice," he tells her, twisting his mouth into a mocking frown. "His tastes run more toward pain than pleasure. Inflicting it, especially."

Six lets out another strangled half-sob. I don't think she's faking it this time. This has gone far enough. I turn to look at Tank, trying to signal to him. It's time to get her out of here.

But before I can, all hell breaks loose.

"I'll enjoy breaking you in myself," Ellis murmurs with a leer. "In fact, I think I'll take a little sample right now." He reaches for her, one arm wrapping around her waist, the other reaching between her legs and up her skirt. He pulls her against him, mouth coming down roughly on hers. Six lets out a muffled scream, then pushes him away, leg coming up instinctively to knee him in the groin. As soon as she connects, Ellis roars in pain and surprise. He half-doubles over, his face a mask of rage. Then, raising his ringed hand, he hauls back and backhands her in the face.

Almost before my brain registers it, I snap. I close the distance between me and my former stepfather and punch him so hard he flies backward into the bearded guy. It happens so fast, his men are taken totally off-guard. But the Lords have been waiting for Tank's signal, so they're ready. Striker's pistol is out and he punches one of the other men with it, knocking him to the ground. Beside him, Tweak shoots another in the leg. He screams, stumbling, and starts to reach for his own gun, but Tweak puts another bullet in his chest. I dive for Ellis, and out of the corner of my eye I see Six is on the ground. I pray she's not hurt.

I send Ellis crashing to the floor. The beast inside me takes control and I grab his head and slam it against the cement floor, hearing a solid crack. Then again. He's out cold after the third time. I leap to my feet just in time to help Tank, who's wrestling one of the others for control of a pistol. I punch him hard in the kidney, then haul him upright. He doubles over and starts to retch. The pistol skitters away.

"Bullet!" Striker yells out. I turn just in time for a fist to connect with my temple. I let out a roar and bend forward, head down, taking the motherfucker in the gut and snow-plowing him until we're both on the ground. One hard punch to the jaw dazes him long enough for me to take out my Glock. Aiming at his chest, I pull the trigger.

Scrambling to my feet, I swing around, eyes scanning the room to assess the scene. Tweak, Lug Nut, Tank and Striker are all on their feet. Ellis's men are on the ground, either unconscious or dead. My brothers are staring at a spot behind me. I turn to look.

There, face bloodied and swollen, Six is holding a gun. Pointed at Ellis.

Blood is streaming from her nose, her lip split and swelling as I take the pistol from her shaking hands and give it to Tank. Already, a bloom of purple is spreading across her cheekbone.

"Are you okay?" I ask, my voice hoarse and strange.

Six nods mutely.

My hand reaches up, but I stop short of touching her, afraid I'll hurt her. Instead, I turn to Tweak.

"Take her back to the limo," I choke.

Six looks at me, eyes wide. She doesn't utter a word, casting one final glance down at Ellis as Tweak leads her away. There's nothing for her to say. She knows what's about to happen. The bare bones of it, anyway.

But I'm hoping she can't see on my face how much I'm going to enjoy it.

ONCE ELLIS REALIZES no one is coming to save his ass, it doesn't take much to get him to spill everything he knows about the rich client he was trying to buy Six for. I guess he figures it's his only shot at getting out of this alive. He hasn't changed at all in that respect: always willing to sell anyone else down the river to save his own skin.

But when all is said and done, and he realizes it isn't going to be enough — that the whole thing has been a set-up to smoke him out of his fucking hole— I finally get the first taste of the revenge I've been craving for so long.

"Go grab the containers from the back of the limo," I tell Lug Nut.

The look of terror in Ellis's eyes as I pull off my beard is a sight I'll never fucking forget.

But that's nothing compared to the look on his face when Lug returns, carrying two large gas cans.

"You got my mother hooked on meth," I rasp at him.

Ellis struggles against his bonds. "She was a fuckin' drunk when I met her," he shoots back. "I didn't make her an addict. I just gave her what she wanted."

"She burned to death in that house because of you." I lean down until my face is less than a foot from his. Close enough that I know he can see the hatred blazing in my eyes. "I've been waiting for this moment for a long fucking time, Ellis."

At first, he doesn't say anything. Then, he starts begging for his life.

I hardly fucking hear him.

"Tie him up." I command.

"NO!" Ellis screams, his eyes bugging wildly out of his head.

Lug Nut and Striker bind his hands and feet, Striker punching him in the face when he starts to struggle too much. They line a couple of the sawhorses up side by side so the tops make a sort of stretcher. Then they haul Ellis up so he's lying on top of them, and secure him there with the last of the rope. Tank stands impassively next to the two gas cans, arms crossed, watching.

When they're finished, I step up to the sawhorses, until I'm looking down on my former stepfather, like a surgeon gazing at a patient on an operating table.

"You never fucking cared about my mom, did you?" I ask, staring him in the eyes. "I bet you thought you'd given me the slip. I'll admit, it's taken me a while to find your ass. Hell, you might have thought you were safe by now." I reach to my waist and unbuckle my belt, slipping it out of the loops of my jeans. Ellis continues to struggle as I wrap it around his left forearm, pulling it tight. "But I would have looked for you until the day I died, if that's what it took."

When the makeshift tourniquet is secure, I reach into my pocket, and pull out a vial and a syringe.

"Hold him still," I tell Tank and Striker.

Then, as Ellis continues to kick and scream, I fill the syringe. The vein in his forearm isn't hard to find. I shove the needle in, pull back the plunger, and see the telltale red of blood. Loosening the belt, I slowly inject the meth.

It's probably not quite enough to kill him, but I can't be sure. That's the one flaw in my plan. If he's lucky, he'll stroke out and die before I want him to.

His eyes roll back into his head for a second. Not long after that, he starts trying to scream again, but little by little his breathing becomes labored. He yells for help, yells that he doesn't want to die, but eventually the words he screams stop making any sense — and pretty soon they're no longer words at all, just animal cries of terror.

When the seizures start, I nod at Striker and Tank. They each grab a gas can. The sweet, acrid aroma of gasoline fills the air as they pour it out onto every flammable surface — dousing the walls, the cords of wood, and Ellis himself. Tank uses the last liquid in his can to make a trail from the center of the barn to the door. We walk out, and once we're outside, I pull out a matchbook, light it, and toss it inside.

The limo isn't behind the pole barn anymore. Tweak drove it down to the end of the drive, at my direction. I didn't want Six to see or hear any of this. Striker, Tank, and Lug Nut walk down to the vehicle, boots crunching in the gravel.

I stay a while. To listen, until the roar of the flames drowns out Ellis's screams.

When it finally does, I put my hands in the pockets of my jacket. Underneath my clothing, I know, is the bullet tattoo Six inked into my skin.

And next to it, the hellhound. The bearer of death.

Fire cleanses. I've heard that said many times in my life. But now I understand what it means.

I feel cleaner than I have in a long time. The weight of my anger and hatred — the weight of the past — has been lifted.

Now it's time to go back to the woman I love. And put the past to rest.

I have a lot to say to Six when we get back to Tanner Springs.

And the first thing is:

I'm sorry.

SIX

The six of us spend the trip back to Tanner Springs mostly in silence. I have questions about what happened back at the pole barn after Tweak led me away, but I'm not sure I want to ask any of them.

"You doin' okay?" Bullet murmurs a couple of times as he drives, his eyes never leaving the road.

"I'm fine," I assure him, gnawing at a hangnail on my thumb as I stare out the window.

"How's your face?" Tweak asks from behind me.

"Feeling kind of puffy," I admit. "My nose has stopped bleeding, though."

"You did good back there, you know that, Stacia?" Tank calls from the back. It's strange to know them all well enough now that I recognize their voices so easily. "Bullet was right to trust you. If it wasn't for you, we wouldn't have got Edge today."

"I'd do it again," I say, and I realize it's true. "It was a little scary, I'll admit. But I'd do anything for Bullet."

The words are out of my mouth before realize what I've said. My cheeks flush hot. I hunker down in the passenger seat and look back out the side window so I don't have to see his reaction.

When we get to the clubhouse, I'm surprised to see not only a bunch of the Lords of Carnage men, but also a handful of women there, too. Sam is there, as well as Kylie and Jewel, whom I recognize from the Smiling Skull. There's also a beautiful redhead who looks familiar, and I realize I think she owns the coffee shop downtown.

Sam rushes over and throws her arms around me, looking relieved. "I knew you'd all be fine, but I wanted to be here when you got back, all the same." She scrutinizes my face anxiously. "What happened to you?"

"Nothing too bad," I assure her. "I just got sort of... punched, I guess." I start to laugh, realizing how odd that must sound. But it's all starting to fade away, and seem less than real at this point.

That said, I'm really looking forward to things in my life calming down a little bit.

"Come on and meet the rest of the women." Sam leads me over to the group of them, who are all standing around in a circle. Jewel and Kylie greet me with warm hugs. The redhead introduces herself as Sydney, and points to a man named Brick across the room, saying she's his wife. Next to her, a blonde and a brunette who must be sisters introduce themselves as Alix and Eden.

"I'm with Gunner, over there," says Alix. "And Eden is with Lug Nut, who you already know."

"Oh, yes!" I murmur, realizing Eden is the woman who the Lords rescued from a man who got her hooked on heroin. I'm not about to bring that up, of course, but I can't help but steal a few looks at her as the women chat excitedly around me. She's gorgeous, her fine features giving her a fragile look. She seems less extraverted than Eden, but her mannerisms echo those of her sister, which is fun to watch. She looks happy, too. I catch her glancing over at Lug Nut a few times, and it doesn't take a genius to notice the obvious love between them.

"We're planning a big barbecue this weekend, here at the clubhouse," Jewel says, cutting through the chatter. She gives me a warm smile. "I hope you'll be able to make it."

"I mean... I'm not sure," I falter. "Doesn't Bullet have to invite me?"

Jewel snorts and rolls her eyes, but not unkindly. "He will," she smirks. "And even if he doesn't, I'm inviting you. As the wife of the MC president, my word is law." She wiggles her eyebrows as the other women laugh.

"In that case, I accept your invitation," I chuckle, knowing I'll only show up if Bullet wants me to.

Eventually, I stop being the topic of conversation among the women, and I manage to slip out to the back room where Sam did my photo session that day. I grab the backpack I brought with me and change out of my skirt and platforms, into some jeans and low-heeled boots. I go into the bathroom and take a look at my face, grimacing at my split, puffy lip. There's some bruising on my cheekbone and around my eye, but it's not as bad as I thought it would be. I run some cold water, dab the blood off, and splash my face until it feels a little better.

When I come back out into the main room of the clubhouse, Bullet immediately catches my eye and comes striding over to me. "I was looking for you," he frowns. His face still has that concerned look he's been wearing for the past couple of hours.

"I just went to change and freshen up," I explain.

He nods. "You about ready to head out, then?"

I suppress a wave of disappointment. I'm guessing his plan is to take me home. Which means this might be over. But I'm not going to ask him about it, or beg him to spend the night with me. He helped me, and then I helped him. That might be the extent of it. And if it is, that's just something I'll have to accept.

"Sure," I say in a small voice. "I'll go get my stuff."

Once we're outside, I pull my backpack over both shoulders and climb onto Bullet's bike behind him. As he starts the engine, I wrap my arms around his torso. I breathe him in, closing my eyes at how familiar and heady the scent of him is. Soon we're flying down the highway, toward a chapter of my life that suddenly seems like more of a blank page than ever.

We've been riding a few minutes when suddenly Bullet lets out a loud curse. "Goddamnit!" he shouts into the wind.

Startled, I shift in my seat and lean forward a little. "What is it?"

But he doesn't answer. Instead, he pulls off the road onto the gravel shoulder and stops the bike. He cuts the engine, and, not knowing what else to do, I climb off.

"Bullet..." I begin in a worried voice as he swings his leg over the bike, but he cuts me off.

"I'm not gonna put this off one more damn minute," he growls. He reaches up and grasps me by both shoulders. "Six, I'm so fucking sorry. Because of me, you could have gotten killed earlier today. I will never fucking forgive myself for putting you in that kind of danger."

"Don't do that, Bullet. We've already been through this," I counter. "You tried to stop me. But short of actually locking me away in a room, you weren't going to talk me out of it. You saved me from Flash's enemies. And I helped you get to your stepfather. We're even." I search his gorgeous, tormented face. "Please stop apologizing," I beg. "I wanted to do it. I don't regret a thing." I pause. "I meant what I said earlier. I'd do it all again. I would have done anything to help you."

Bullet's eyes lock on mine. "You know I killed him."

I nod. "I know. And I also know you wouldn't have done it if you didn't have a reason."

"You're right." He leans against the bike, sitting down on the seat, and pulls me to him. "And it's about time I explain to you what that reason was. You deserve that much."

And so he does.

He tells me about his mom. About her horrific death, and how he's spent years looking for his stepfather to make him pay for it. I listen in horror, my heart aching with pain, as Bullet tells me everything. His anger, and sorrow, and guilt. The dreams of vengeance that drove him for so long. The blackness that ate at his soul.

"It kept me from ever getting close to anyone else." He stares at me, eyes deep and dark with emotion. "Until you."

My heart starts to ricochet in my chest.

"Until me," I whisper, hardly wanting to let myself believe my ears.

"Yes. Until you," he murmurs, drawing me close. "Until I met this blond spitfire at a tattoo parlor, who was even more closed off than I was. Somewhere along the line, I got so caught up in getting you to loosen up around me that I forgot to keep myself walled off from you.

I pull in a ragged breath. "You were pretty persistent," I risk.

"There was just something about you I couldn't stay away from. Something in your eyes that pulled me to you. Until I was bound and determined to get past all those walls you kept throwing up to protect yourself. You pulled me out of myself." He pauses. "By the time I figured out what was going on, I was too far gone. That's part of the reason I stopped you from changing the eye on the hellhound tattoo."

By now I'm trying like hell not to start crying. "I don't get what you mean," I manage to say, shaking my head.

Bullet reaches up with one hand and gently touches my non-bruised cheek. "I wanted the hellhound in the first place because it's a symbol of vengeance," he tells me. "A symbol of the revenge that was driving me to find Ellis. To make him pay for what he had done." He pauses, frowning slightly. "There you were, putting ink on me that you didn't know the meaning of. The only truly good, innocent thing in my life. And then, when you messed up his eye and made it a heart... Fuck, I dunno. It was weird. It felt right somehow. Like it wasn't a mistake after all, since it was you who put it there. Maybe it was a glimmer of something more in my life. Something better. A window to the other side."

He bends down and gives me a soft kiss on my forehead. "I fuckin' love that you're the one who put that ink on me, Six. That little heart, that no one will ever know is there, except me and you? It means something. It means the end of the bad chapters in both of our lives. And the beginning of something new for us. Together."

My heart is racing. This is so much more than I expected — so much more than I had hoped for — that I feel a little dizzy. "I never would have pegged you for a romantic," I tell him, shell-shocked

"Neither would I, babe," he chuckles. "Believe me. But you've changed me."

"I think you've changed me, too," I breathe as he pulls me against him. We stay like that, my face against his warm, solid chest, breathing in the cooling air of nightfall. I know already that this is a moment that will remain etched in my memory, probably for the rest of my life.

After a moment, Bullet clears his throat.

"So, I know people are starting to call you Stacia now," he rumbles. "But if it's okay with you, I think I'm gonna keep callin' you Six."

I pull away to look up at his face. His eyes are twinkling.

"Why?" I ask him.

"Because. It reminds me of something."

I snort and roll my eyes. "Okay, really? Way to ruin the romantic moment. Just so you know, Bullet, you've given me a lot more than six orgasms by now."

"Believe me, I'm well aware," he murmurs. "But that's not exactly it. There's one time in particular that stands out. It was number six, as a matter of fact. But not for the reason you think."

"Why then?" I ask, amused. "Or should I be afraid to ask?"

"It's because that was the night I realized I wasn't ready to let you go after six orgasms. Or six days. Or even six months." He leans down and brushes his lips with mine. "I think that was the night I started fallin' head over heels in love with you."

For a few seconds I'm speechless with astonishment.

"What did you say?" I finally manage to whisper.

"You heard me. I'm in love with you. You've always been mine, Stacia. Since the day I first saw you at Rebel Ink." Bullet brushes my hair aside and kisses the rose tattoo on my neck. I suppress a moan at the contact of his lips on my skin. "You were sexy, and sassy, and closed off as hell. Thorny, tough, and beautiful. Just like this rose. You were made for me. And I'm pretty sure you know it, too."

My throat starts to ache as a sob bubbles up, but it comes out as a happy laugh instead. "Oh, you do, do you?" I tease, tears spilling out of my eyes before I can stop them.

Bullet reaches up with a thumb and brushes them off my cheek. "Don't fight it, babe. It's stronger than either one of us, lord knows."

"That's my middle name," I blurt out.

"What?" He furrows his brow, confused.

"Rose is my middle name," I say, reaching up to touch the spot where the flower adorns my skin. It feels so good to tell him this. To tell him about things no one else knows but me, and now him.

"I got this tattoo after I ran away for the first time," I explain. "After I stopped using my real name, I still wanted some connection to it. So that I wouldn't feel like I was disappearing, you know? But I couldn't get a tattoo that said 'Stacia'. It would have been too risky. And besides, who tattoos their own name on their body?" I lean into Bullet, savoring the warmth of him, the solid strength of his arms around me. "So I chose a rose instead. It was like a private joke between me and myself — a secret that only I knew. My message to myself that I was still me. It gave me hope that someday I'd be able to be me again."

"And here you are," Bullet murmurs. "You again. My Mystery Girl isn't a mystery anymore. My Stacia Rose."

His lips cover mine. I kiss him back. Desperately, fervently, madly. Because he's right.

I'm done running. I'm done fighting. I'm not a mystery anymore. And I am his. All his.

I'm staying in Tanner Springs, with Bullet. And as our tongues dance, I'm sure he can hear the word ringing in my head, pumping through my heart. Through every vein and every cell in my body.

Yes. Yes!

The sound of a honking horn startles us, breaking us apart. As I open my eyes, a pickup truck flies by us on the highway, the wind wake from its passing lifting my hair from my shoulders. From the rolled-down windows, a couple of male voices catcall and hoot at us. An arm shoots out and waves a cowboy hat, as its owner shouts something that I can't quite make out.

"I think they told us to get a room," I murmur, blushing.

"I got a better idea," Bullet chuckles. He gives me one more long, dizzying kiss, then lets go of me.

"Oh yeah?"

He straddles the bike, then winks at me and motions for me to get on. "Yeah. My place."

EPILOGUE
BULLET

Several months later

"Oh, wait!" Six cries, turning back toward the car. "We almost forgot the flowers!"

I watch as she runs over to where we've parked, at the edge of the small gravel alley. She's wearing a modest black dress I've never seen on her before, and an understated pair of ballet flats. Even in that, she looks gorgeous, and sexy as hell. Just like always.

I had picked Six up at the end of her shift at Rebel Ink this afternoon to drive down here to the cemetery. She insisted that we stop back home first so she could change into something 'more appropriate' than what she wore to work. I almost told her not to bother. After all, the dead aren't around anymore to judge. But truth be told, I'm kind of touched she's taking this so seriously.

Six comes back with the flowers — a colorful bouquet of spring blooms and daisies she picked out at the florist. The two of us walk together toward the plot, with me leading the way. I've only been here once before, but I still remember exactly where it is.

I come to a stop in front of the simple, unremarkable square grave stone that marks my mother's final resting place. Six moves to stand next to me, and I take her hand. I watch as she silently reads the simple inscription: *Carol Ann Lamarr.*

"Thank you for bringing me here," Six whispers.

"Thanks for wanting to come."

"I wish I could have met her."

I pause for a second, contemplating how to answer.

"The drugs had taken over most of who she was," I say slowly. "If you'd met her toward the end, you probably wouldn't have liked her much. But the mom I remember from when I was a little kid was funny and nice. Spontaneous. She'd be cooking dinner, and all of a sudden, she'd turn on the radio and make me start dancing with her to whatever song was playing."

I smile at the memory, wondering where it came from. It's been years since I've thought about the way my mother was early on. The good mom. The one who loved me more than she loved drugs and booze. The one who tried like hell to get by in the world — to get us both a better life, before life wore her out.

I feel Six's eyes on me. "What else do you remember about her?" she asks.

I think for a moment. "Her favorite color was green. She

loved German chocolate cake. She made me breakfast for dinner whenever I asked for it."

"That's sweet. She sounds like a good person. A good mother."

I nod, as a painful, unexpected lump forms in my throat.

"Yeah," I say gruffly. "She was."

We stay for a little while like that, Six's small hand resting in mine. I tell her some of the other things I remember about my mother. And then, we stop talking, each of us lost in our own thoughts. I'm not a praying man, but even so, I find myself talking to my mom in my head. I tell her I'm sorry I didn't manage to get her away from Ellis. I tell her about Six, and how somehow she found a tiny crack in my black heart, and pried it open to let the sun shine in.

I tell her I've learned that sometimes, two damaged people can find each other and heal together.

Eventually, Six kneels down and gently places the bouquet of flowers in front of the grave stone. "Goodbye, Ms. Lamarr," she says in a quiet voice.

Bye, Mom, I say in my head. *I'm sorry I couldn't stop your demons from catching up with you. But I'll do my best to help Six help her own mom. And I'll give you the only second chance I can. I'll remember you the way you were before the drugs took you. The best version of you will live on in my memory.*

And I won't let that version die. I promise.

IN THE END, Six decided she couldn't keep the jewels.

An associate of our club checked them out, and confirmed that none of them were registered. Tweak couldn't find any records of thefts from the past ten years that matched the description of them, either. There was no way to find out who they came from, and no way to give them back.

But even though Six was in the clear, she still didn't want the money she could make from them.

"Turning them in to the police doesn't make any sense, darlin'," I told her when we talked it over. "They'll just sit on a shelf somewhere. Or more likely, some crooked cop will take them for himself and sell them."

"I know," she admitted. "But I don't feel right profiting from them, either. I'd always know whatever money we got was tainted."

So, the envelope with the diamonds, emeralds, and topaz sat in the bottom of my gun safe for a couple of months, while Six tried to decide what to do with them.

Eventually, a solution came to her on its own.

One night, as the two of us were lying on the couch after a marathon session of sex, Six's cell phone rang. It was her mom. She was crying, and desperate, and she told Six that she was out of money, sick, and needed help getting sober once and for all. She begged Six to come see her, and to help her find a program that could get her off the booze.

She and her mom talked for over an hour, while I just sat and held her. At first, Six's voice was flat, guarded. But after a while, I heard it start to soften. Every so often, a tear would slip down one of her cheeks.

By the time Six hung up, she was full-on crying. She turned to me, her eyes shiny and bright, and gave me a tremulous smile full of hope.

"I know what the jewels are for now," she whispered.

Six used the money from selling the jewels to check her mom into a three-month-long inpatient rehab program. When she got out, she moved here to Tanner Springs, into Six's apartment — to be away from her triggers, and close to her only daughter.

And Six moved into my place with me.

Her mom's been out of rehab for about two months now. So far, it seems to be taking.

Six started working full time as a tattoo artist at Rebel Ink around the same time her mom went into rehab. She's quickly become one of the most popular and asked-for artists in the shop. I'm fucking proud of her. But even more important than that, it means she's gonna stick around for a while. Which makes me happy as hell.

And there's one more sign of that. One she just showed me tonight.

WHEN WE GET BACK to our place after visiting the cemetery, Six sinks down on the couch and removes her shoes. "Oh, man," Six moans as she massages one of her feet. "My feet are killing me, as is my neck." She rocks her head from side to side and does a few circles with her shoulders. "It's amazing how hard on your body doing ink can be."

"Well, you better get over it and start making my dinner, woman," I joke.

Six just snorts and shoots me a look. "Good damn thing you aren't serious right now."

"Not at all. Wanna order pizza or something?"

"How about that Mexican place that delivers? I'd love some pork tacos. "

"Done."

I place the call and order an obscene fuckin' amount of grub. Just after I hang up, Six pulls herself up off the couch. "I'm going to go take a quick shower before the food gets here."

"You want company?"

Six starts to nod, but then frowns. "Someone should probably wait for the delivery guy," she says, looking regretful.

I shrug. "That doesn't stop me from coming in and watching."

But strangely, Six purses her lips instead of agreeing. "Um, how about I take a rain check? By the way, I have a surprise for you a little later."

"A surprise, eh?" She nods, and the coy look in her eyes makes me instantly hard. "I hope it's what I think it is."

"You'll just have to find out," she teases me.

Six goes into the bathroom and shuts the door. "Don't come in!" she says in a muffled yell as I hear the shower start. It's weird, and I'd almost be worried if I didn't know Six so well by now. Instead I just shrug and go grab a beer, then settle in to wait for the food to get here.

About ten minutes later, the door opens and she comes out in a pair of yoga pants and one of my shirts. Her hair is up in a loose mess on top of her head, a few tendrils falling around her face. The sight of her sends a lightning bolt straight to my dick. But before I can act on it, the doorbell rings, and the food arrives.

We eat dinner sitting on the couch. I pull up a stupid TV series we've been watching, but we never actually press play because we're too busy talking and getting caught up with each other's days before we drove out to the cemetery. I tell her how Gunner and Thorn convinced Tweak some random-ass bruise he's got on his arm means he's probably got testicular cancer. Six snorts with laughter until she's afraid food's going to come out her nose. She tells me about a couple of lovebirds barely out of high school who came in to get matching tattoos with each other's initials and a heart. Chance tried to talk them out of it, but they wouldn't take no for an answer. In the end, though, the boy got so freaked out by the sight of the tattoo gun that he passed out cold. So their skin remains unmarred for the time being.

"Good thing," I grin. "That's gotta be near the top of the list of most regretted tattoos. You'd think people would know better."

"Yeah," Six agrees. "But still, you never can tell. Maybe those two will be together forever. High school sweethearts last sometimes."

"True." I chuckle. "But judging from your story, one thing they'll never have is matching ink."

"So..." Six says slowly. "Speaking of that. I think maybe it's time to show you my surprise."

And then, I finally find out why she didn't want me in the shower with her earlier.

Six reaches down and lifts up one corner of the oversized T-shirt she's wearing. I see a flash of white on her right side, just below her ribs, and realize it's a bandage.

"Pull it off," Six directs me, "but try to be gentle with the tape."

I do as she says, noticing that she's holding her breath as I peel away the adhesive from her skin.

Underneath, a new tattoo appears.

It's a bullet, piercing through the hole of a number six.

Apart from the fact that it sort of matches mine, the meaning of it is instantly clear: I've pierced through her defenses. I've gotten through to what's underneath.

"Chance did it," Six murmurs. "Since I'm not quite badass enough to do my own tats. You like it?"

For a moment, I can't talk. When I can, my voice comes out kind of fucked up and wobbly.

"So, looks like you're feeling pretty confident this thing between us is gonna last," I say, trying to sound nonchalant.

"Yeah." Her eyes shine as they meet mine. "I'm feeling pretty good about it."

"Good damn thing." I replace the bandage and carefully slide my finger along the tape to reseal it. "'Cause I've got a little surprise of my own."

I get up off the couch and go into the bedroom, where I've hidden the cut that says I've claimed her in a bag on a high shelf. When I bring it out, she exclaims in happiness and quickly stands so I can put it on her. She wears it proudly for the rest of the night — until it comes off, along with the T-shirt, the yoga pants, and the rest of it when I take her to bed.

"Bullet," she moans as I enter her from behind. She's on her knees in front of me, giving me a perfect view of the curve of her gorgeous fucking ass. Her long blond hair is thrown over one shoulder, and her shapely neck arches back as she meets me thrust for thrust. Six is wet and hot, her pussy clenching my cock as I bury myself deep. Reaching around with one hand, I slide my palm around her breast, my thumb grazing her hardened nipple. She moans again, her hips bucking slightly.

"That's right, baby," I murmur as my cock pulses inside her. "Fuck yes, that's good."

My hand leaves her breast and travels south, finding the slick heat of her clit. Her juices coat my fingers as I slide one lightly over the taut skin. Six gasps and bucks again, the gasp ending in a soft cry. I feel her contract around me. I pull out and thrust, savoring it as long as I can. The hand that's grasping her hip pulls her backwards into me as I go deeper, harder. She's with me, wanting it as she arches her back and opens more for me. Growling, knowing I can't take much more, I slide my finger along her pulsing nub again, and that's all it takes. Six cries out, and as she does I speed up my rhythm, loving the way her pussy contracts, pulling me in, milking me, and then two seconds later I shout her name and lose myself inside her, coming so hard I see stars.

"Bullet," she gasps as we continue to rock together, riding the wave that we've created. "I love you. I love this. I'm so lucky."

But I know I'm the lucky one.

Six is the most amazing woman I've ever known. Loving her gives me the determination of a hundred men. I would kill for her again in a heartbeat. I would die for her. With her in my life, I've never been stronger. And I know that will only grow with time. We'll be together forever. Six has always been mine.

And she always will be.

DAPHNE TALKS OUT HER ASS ABOUT BULLET

BULLET started out as a novella called *Rebel Ink*, which came out in a USA Today Bestselling anthology called *Wanted: An Outlaw Anthology*. The anthology came out in January 2019, and it was only available for a month or so, which was always the intent. It was a charity anthology to make money for Saint Jude Children's Hospital. We ended up raising $5,400 for Saint Jude, and I'm extremely proud of all the authors who contributed their blood, sweat, and tears for it.

At the time, I figured that once the anthology was unpublished, I would probably just release *Rebel Ink* as-is as a standalone novella, so that anyone who hadn't read it in the anthology could get it. But the thing was, once I had written about Bullet and Six, I fell in love with them both, and it just bugged me that their story didn't get a full-length novel like the rest of the Lords of Carnage men. So I put off releasing *Rebel Ink* as it was... and after a couple of months, an idea for a separate MC plot line came to me that would show readers more of what was happening in Bullet's MC world during the time he was trying to help Six. The result is this book.

I hope you love Bullet and Six's story, and that you're excited to see what happens in the next Lords of Carnage series. There will be three more full-length novels in this original LOC series... and Tank's story is next!

BOOKS BY DAPHNE LOVELING

Motorcycle Club Romance

Los Perdidos MC
Fugitives MC
Throttle: A Stepbrother Romance
Rush: A Stone Kings Motorcycle Club Romance
Crash: A Stone Kings Motorcycle Club Romance
Ride: A Stone Kings Motorcycle Club Romance
Stand: A Stone Kings Motorcycle Club Romance
GHOST: Lords of Carnage MC
HAWK: Lords of Carnage MC
BRICK: Lords of Carnage MC
GUNNER: Lords of Carnage MC
THORN: Lords of Carnage MC
BEAST: Lords of Carnage MC
ANGEL: Lords of Carnage MC
HALE: Lords of Carnage MC
Dirty Santa (Novella)
IRON WILL: Lords of Carnage Ironwood MC
IRON HEART: Lords of Carnage Ironwood MC

Sports Romance

Getting the Down: A Bad Boy Sports Romance
Snap Count: A Bad Boy Sports Romance
Zone Blitz: A Bad Boy Sports Romance

Paranormal Romance

Untamed Moon

Daphne Loveling is a small-town girl who moved to the big city as a young adult in search of adventure. She lives in the American Midwest with her fabulous husband and the two cats who own them.

Someday, she hopes to retire to a sandy beach and continue writing with sand between her toes.

Made in the USA
Coppell, TX
10 May 2020